THE NUMBER GAME

A SAMMY & BRIAN MYSTERY #8

BY KEN MUNRO

GASLIGHT PUBLISHERS

The Number Game

Copyright © 1998
by Ken Munro

All rights reserved.

Gaslight Publishers
P. O. Box 258
Bird-in-Hand, PA 17505

E-mail: sammybrian@desupernet.net

Library of Congress Number: 98-68031
International Standard Book Number: 1-883294-75-4

Printed 1998 by
Masthof Press
220 Mill Road
Morgantown, PA 19543-9701

THE NUMBER GAME

PROLOGUE

The gloomy weather would only add to the confusion of what was about to happen. Rain was not in the forecast, but red lightning was about to strike.

The old man carrying the briefcase was in a hurry. He glanced up at the gray clouds. It was unusually hot for May. Perspiration was beading on his forehead and sticking to his underarms. He was on the alert. It went with his job.

He surveyed the pedestrians headed in his direction. Ten feet away was a thin, middle-aged man carrying a bag of groceries. The old man watched as the bag slipped from the man's hands, hit the sidewalk, and split open. The thin man bent down to retrieve his spilled food. As the old man approached to offer help, he was caught off guard. A ketchup bottle was pointed at his face.

His right hand released the briefcase and joined his other hand in protecting himself from the squirting ketchup. It was too late. The red paste landed in his hair, on his face, and clung to his suit.

Just as fast and surprising, a figure emerged from behind and grabbed the briefcase.

The action that played itself out came so suddenly. So unexpectedly. The onlookers gasped in disbelief. They stood there dumbfounded as their minds tried to accept what had happened. It was during this period of confusion that the stranger had snatched up the briefcase and entered a nearby car.

In seconds the car was gone. The stranger was gone. The briefcase was gone. One million dollars in diamonds was gone.

CHAPTER ONE

*F*ourteen months later.

    The Tuesday afternoon crowd had finally settled down at the Conestoga Auction. The first thirty minutes had had people drifting in and out. Several had been socializing, impatiently waiting for their items of interest to come up for bid. But with a little scolding from the auctioneer, the noise subsided. Now that the auctioneer had everyone's attention, the bidding soon drifted into a predictable pattern. The latecomer who barged into the back of the room caused a few heads to turn, but most eyes concentrated on the next article being put up for bid.

    Jeff DeHart, the auctioneer, sat on a raised platform. The next item put up for sale was a piece of pottery. He inspected the vase closely to evaluate its condition. A few small nicks and a hairline crack marred the otherwise handsome vase. Only a professional collector would recognize it for what it was. The simple markings of its design would render it junk to some people and "interesting" to others. But to a serious collector, its irregular design held a fascination.

"This vase is chipped here and here," said the auctioneer, pointing to the small v-shaped nicks around the neck. There's also a small crack down the side." He leaned over, reached down, and took a framed picture from Gordon Wolgemuth who was in charge of handing articles from the nearby table to the auctioneer.

The frame around the crudely painted picture was worth more than the amateurish painting itself. Jeff noted the name of the painter in the lower right-hand corner. "Sidney Thomas is the artist," he announced to the crowd.

A soft rumble of voices spread across the room.

The eighteen- by twenty-four-inch painting showed two men playing a game of dominoes. Jeff DeHart tried to find some redeeming quality in the artwork. He found none. His eyebrows lifted, but he tried not to show his dislike for the picture. "Two for one money," he said as he displayed both the vase and the painting side by side.

"Okay, lot number 427, two pieces, a vase and a painting. Who will give five dollars? Five, three. Who'll give three dollars? Three, three, three."

A bidder, seen only by the auctioneer, raised a finger and mouthed the word one. A bidding paddle with the number 54 lay on his lap.

"One dollar I have," announced the auctioneer. "Now two, two. Who'll give two dollars?" he asked, handing the two items back down to Gordon to hold and display closer to the audience.

A paddle in the far back, showing the number 101, jutted up. Holding the paddle was the late arrival, who had settled into an empty seat in the last row. He was a small, thin man in his forties. The image he projected was that of a loser. His sunken eyes, creased-lined face, and a perpetual frown indicated years of low self-esteem. His quick entrance into the room and his energy laden paddle were the only signs that something had recently motivated Mr. 101.

"I have two dollars. Who'll give me three? Three, three. Three I have," said Jeff, acknowledging Mr. 54.

"Five!" responded a desperate voice from the back row, Mr. 101.

"Five. I have five from the back. Who will make it seven?" asked Jeff DeHart.

"Seven," came the firm voice of Mr. 54.

"Ten," said the impatient Mr. 101, who appeared to be a man on a mission.

It was at this point in the action that Sammy Wilson along with his friend, Brian Helm, started to take a serious interest in the proceedings. The two fifteen-year-old amateur detectives from Bird-in-Hand came periodically to the Conestoga Auction with Sammy's mother. She was always looking for antique quilts to sell in her shop.

Sammy Wilson was usually on the lookout for baseball cards. However, his interest in old baseball cards had declined recently. With the boys' increased detective work in Lancaster County, Sammy had little time to spend in his parents' shop. In fact, when his parents moved their business, The Bird-in-Hand Country Store, across the street, his sports card display case was eliminated.

If Sammy's mind had been on baseball cards when he entered the auction, it wasn't now. The unusual bidding frenzy had changed all that. Something mysterious was going on. Sammy could feel it. He looked again at the vase and the painting. Which of the two items held the answer? he wondered. He twisted to his left and joined Brian, his mother, and the others in a quick glance at the small man in the back row.

"Ten, I have ten. Fifteen. Who'll give fifteen?" asked Jeff DeHart, looking at the two men's faces and knowing from experience that the bidding now warranted unit bids of five dollars instead of one or two. He looked at Mr. 54 and asked again, "Fifteen?"

Mr. 54 nodded back.

"I have fifteen. Give twenty? Who'll give twenty?" asked Jeff, casting his eyes back to Mr. 101, who gave a nervous jerk with his head and paddle.

Gordon, who was holding the vase and the painting, tightened his grip as the bidding increased, thirty, forty, fifty dollars. Disbelief replaced the passive look on his face. He lowered the painting to the floor and allowed it to lean back against his leg. He secured the vase with both hands. He wasn't about to let it fall and break. He glanced again at its imperfections. Fifty dollars, he thought to himself. Why would someone be willing to pay fifty dollars for an old cracked vase?

Sammy and Brian were thinking the same thing as the tension rose in the room.

The auctioneer had increased the bidding by ten dollars. "Sixty. Who'll give sixty?"

With a small nod Mr. 54 indicated he was still interested.

"Seventy. Seventy. Who'll make it seventy?" asked Jeff, seemingly at a loss to explain the unexpected bidding excitement.

From the back, Mr. 101 reluctantly nodded his acceptance of the bid.

"Eighty. Eighty. Now ninety," said Jeff as he acknowledged the nod from Mr. 54 and threw the bidding back to Mr. 101.

Mr. 101 was in deep thought as his paddle lay still on his lap. His left hand made a quick trip to his back pocket that held his wallet. His hand slid over the thin bulge and returned. He shook his head at the auctioneer.

The auctioneer scanned the room. "Ninety? I have eighty. Ninety. Anyone, ninety?"

A new paddle shot up and waved.

Number 28.

"Ninety, I have," said Jeff, his eyes focusing on the newly raised paddle to his far left.

The noise volume in the room increased as heads turned toward the new bidder.

Sammy, Brian, and Mrs. Wilson leaned forward and to their right to get a peek at the person holding paddle 28.

The extra thick, dark glasses the man wore gave him an eerie appearance. The white cane he clutched in his right hand would make one believe the man was blind. His gray thinning hair and wrinkled skin put the man's age at about sixty-five. The blank expression on his face gave the impression he was used to people staring at him.

"One hundred?" asked the auctioneer, again looking at Mr. 54.

Mr. 54 nodded.

"One hundred I have. One hundred twenty-five," said the auctioneer, taking a bold step to test the waters.

The room went quiet. Everyone waited. Electricity was in the air. Gordon was now holding the vase with both hands and had it cushioned against his chest.

"One hundred twenty-five?" Jeff repeated, expecting a reply from Mr. Thick Glasses.

The crowd was not disappointed. Number 28 paddle rose and tilted toward the auctioneer.

"One hundred twenty-five I have," said Jeff. "One hundred fifty. One hundred fifty."

Mr. 54 nodded.

"One hundred fifty, I have."

The noise level increased to the point where Jeff had to remind the crowd to quiet down. Then he resumed the bidding. "One hundred seventy-five. One hundred seventy-five."

Paddle 28 batted the air.

"I have one seventy-five. Two hundred dollars," Jeff announced to Mr. 54.

Again the head nodded.

"Two hundred I have. Two hundred fifty," said Jeff, knowing from the action so far, he would probably get it. Although he couldn't understand why the bidding had escalated to this point.

Brian couldn't stand it any longer. He elbowed his buddy. "There's something valuable hidden in the vase. Right, Sammy?"

"The vase must be a collector's item," said Sammy. "That's the only sense I can make out of all this."

Brian shook his head. "It must be nice to have money to throw away on dust collectors." He then folded his arms across his chest, took a deep breath, closed his eyes, and slouched in his chair.

"Somehow, I don't think that vase will be collecting dust," said Sammy, trying to keep up with the bidding.

"Three hundred I have. Three fifty. Three fifty."

All eyes were on Mr. Thick Glasses.

He remained still. Paddle 28 didn't move. His face showed no signs of reacting to the bid. Instead, he relaxed and smiled.

Was he finished? Why the smile?

"Three fifty," repeated the auctioneer, giving Mr. Thick Glasses a chance to respond.

He didn't.

"Three twenty-five," coaxed Jeff. "Three twenty-five."

Still no response

"Sold to number 54 for three hundred dollars," proclaimed the auctioneer.

Gordon secured the vase with one hand and scooped up the painting with the other. He delivered both items to the owner of paddle 54, who carefully wrapped the vase in newspaper and placed it in a carton. The painting was given no special treatment, just laid across the top of the box.

Sammy glanced over and saw that Mr. 54 stood up and looked at his three full boxes. He nudged Brian who had fallen asleep. "Come on, let's do our good deed for the day."

The constant flowing rhythm of the auctioneer's voice and the mystery surrounding the vase had caused Brian to assume his "secret agent" state of mind. But Sammy's, "Let's do our good deed for the day," slipped Brian from his secret agent mode into a knight ready to battle the dragon. The young princess, crying for help, lay beyond in the dragon's cave. Brian's arms flailed about as he prepared to do his good deed for the day. But as he plunged his sword forward, the dragon disappeared. In its place was a man's face. Brian had poked his finger into the head of the man sitting in front of him.

"Sorry," said Brian as he stood and stumbled after his friend.

Mr. 54, who was quite large and husky, had already picked up one carton as Sammy approached.

"May we help you carry your boxes?" asked Sammy.

"Sure can," replied the man, seeing the two boys he recognized as semi-regulars at the auction. "I'll take one. You bring the others."

The teenage detectives each grabbed a box and followed Mr. 54 outside to his car.

The parking lot was full, but Mr. 54 had evidently arrived early for the auction. His green station wagon was parked right outside the building.

Sammy watched as the man placed one carton on the front passenger seat. The other two he placed in the back of the station wagon. The young detective was willing to bet the box up front contained the vase.

Before the man had a chance to turn around and thank the boys, Sammy said, "May I ask why the vase you bought is so valuable?"

The man turned and smiled. "My wife collects vases that have a history. The vase I got is one of two of a kind. My wife is going to go nuts when she sees the mate to the one she already has."

"How valuable are the vases?" asked Brian.

"Each one by itself is worth about fifty dollars," said the man.

"Only fifty dollars?" said Brian. "But you paid three hundred for it."

The man smiled, finding humor in what Brian had just said. "If someone cut the famous painting Mona Lisa in half and each half was given to a different museum, how much would each half be worth?"

Brian winced at the thought. "The painting would be ruined. You need both pieces to make it whole."

"What you're saying," said Sammy, "is the two vases go together to make a set. To appreciate their full beauty and their history, you must have both vases."

"Right," answered the man as he moved closer to the boys and lowered his voice. "It's the only set of its kind in the world."

"How much are they worth as a pair?" asked Brian.

The man's voice changed to a soft whisper. "Together, the vases are worth ten thousand dollars."

CHAPTER TWO

"**W**ow!" said Brian. "Ten thousand dollars!"

"Let's just keep that to ourselves," said the man.

Both boys nodded.

Sammy raised a closed hand, the thumb pointing to the door. "Does that mean the two men who were bidding against you also know the value of the vase?"

"That's something I can't understand. If my wife has the only other vase, why were they bidding so high for this one?"

"How many people know your wife has the matching vase?" asked Sammy.

"Quite a few, I'm afraid," said the man. "She's been talking about it for months, telling everybody if they see one like it, to let her know."

"So maybe these men thought if they bought the vase for a hundred dollars or so, they could sell it to your wife for a lot more."

"Yeah, could be," said the man. He looked around and then fished a card from his wallet. "Here's my card. If you want to learn more about my wife's vase collecting, give us a call. Mary's always ready to talk about her hobby." He leaned closer to the boys and whispered, "Even more so, now that she has the long lost twin."

Sammy took the business card and glanced at it. The man's name was Paul Brenner. He sold antiques and lived in Leola, a short distance from Bird-in-Hand.

"As you can see, my name is Paul Brenner. And you boys are . . .?"

"I'm Sammy Wilson and this is Brian Helm. We live in Bird-in-Hand."

"Hey, are you the Sammy and Brian who are the amateur detectives?"

Brian stood up straight. "Yes, we are," he replied.

"Well, I'm glad to know you," said Paul, shaking their hands. Then his face lost its smile. He glanced around. "I have to get back in there and return my paddle and pay my bill." He reached into his pocket. "How much do I owe you boys for helping me?"

"You don't owe us anything," replied Sammy. "I always say, 'You're grown up when you stop taking money for helping people.'"

"That's right," added Brian, reluctantly, but he wondered how much Mr. Brenner would have given them if his friend hadn't said anything.

The boys quickened their pace and followed Mr. Brenner back to the building. It was evident he was in a hurry to get the vase home to his wife.

Someone else was also in a hurry. The man was breathing heavily, his eyes darting here and there. He was hiding behind one of the many vehicles parked in the large lot. He couldn't wait to get his hands on the loot. He made his move as Sammy, Brian, and Paul Brenner disappeared back into the Conestoga Auction building. His whole body trembled as he approached the green station wagon. He had already waited a year. That was long enough. One million dollars, thought the man, and now I don't have to share it with anyone.

Later, when Sammy, Brian, and Mrs. Wilson went to the office window to pay her bill, they heard of the incident that had happened in the parking lot. Someone had tried to break into a green station wagon. Luckily, someone was nearby and had chased the man away.

Sammy looked back over the crowd. Mr. Thick Glasses was gone. So was the frail Mr. 101. Had one of them tried to steal the vase? Sammy's thoughts traveled in several directions. He frowned. If someone was desperate enough to attempt to burglarize a car, he thought, then maybe . . . The young detective made a mental note to call Paul Brenner in the morning—or would that be too late?

CHAPTER THREE

The July morning sun battled the quilt for possession of its colors. Now that the Fourth of July had come and gone, the Amish quilt, hanging on the front porch, regained its status as the flag of Amish Country. The pieces of cloth sewed together in distinctive colors and designs were accepted for their simplicity and quality. These standards were natural to the Amish.

The old house displaying the quilt was home to Sammy Wilson and his parents. Another building next to Sammy's home had once been an auto repair garage. With renovations, it became two shops—The Bird-in-Hand Junction and The Bird-in-Hand Country Store. Sammy's grandparents operated the Junction. His parents ran The Bird-in-Hand Country Store. The Amish quilt that accented the porch was an example of hundreds that decorated beds and quilt racks inside the shop.

By ten o'clock, cars, trucks, and campers claimed squatters' rights to most of the parking areas in the little village of Bird-in-Hand. Some tourists hurriedly mapped out a strategy. They planned each step of their visit. They didn't want to waste any of their valuable vacation time. Other tourists adopted the slower, relaxed pace of country life. They went with the simple rhythm of the Amish lifestyle.

Parking space in front of the shops was limited, so Brian leaned his bike against the side of the building. He hurried several steps to the house and banged on the side door. He was on time, and he didn't want to be late. Brian was brought up to believe you should always be at an appointment at least five minutes early. "Hey, Sammy, you in there?" he yelled at the door.

Without losing a beat, the door opened and Sammy came barreling out. Brian stepped back, thinking his friend was going to attack him for yelling.

"Follow me, Brian," said Sammy, heading next door to his parents' shop. "I want you to see something before we go."

"Go? Where are we going?" asked Brian as he followed Sammy into the store.

The aroma of potpourri greeted them inside. Then the smell of cloth and pine took over. More than a thousand bolts of cloth lined the wooden shelves that filled the front half of the store.

You could feel the charm of the old country store. Tourists and locals were already shuffling around the shop, examining the crafts and cloth goods. Amish quilts covered the racks and beds in the back half of the shop.

Brian, who had not been in the shop for several weeks, couldn't believe his eyes. So much cloth in one place. "Wow," was about all he was able to utter as he gawked at all the different patterns that were waiting to become quilts, dresses, aprons, and wall hangings.

"Well, what do you think?" asked Sammy's mother as she poked her head around Lydia Stoltzfus and her daughter Linda to get a better view of the boys.

"Wow!" said Brian. "So this is what quilts look like before they're born."

The two Amish women smiled, turned, and looked at Brian. They wore plain lavender dresses. Their hair was parted in the middle, rolled and wrapped into a bun. A white prayer cap covered the bun. Lydia wore plain black shoes while Linda wore simple sneakers.

To further educate the teenager on quilt-making, Lydia Stoltzfus said, "We used to make our quilts mostly from our old clothes. But that we don't do so much anymore."

"Oh, reincarnation," replied Brian.

Sammy's mother and the two Amish women didn't fully understand Brian's remark, but they smiled anyway.

Sammy appreciated his buddy's metaphor so he added, "That's Brian's way of saying that the cloth once existed as clothing but then came back reincarnated as a quilt."

"We call that recycling," said Lydia Stoltzfus.

Mrs. Wilson smiled. "See, Brian, the Amish keep it simple." She pulled on Lydia's arm, and the women went back to coordinating colors for Lydia's next quilt.

"Come on, Brian. We have something to do," said Sammy as he grabbed his partner and headed for the door.

"Hey, what's up? Where are we going?"

"Remember the antique dealer, Paul Brenner, from yesterday?"

"Yeah," answered Brian.

"He called this morning—after the police left. Somebody broke into his house last night."

"Oh, no. The two vases were stolen. Right, Sammy?"

Sammy and Brian stepped aside as several tourists entered the store.

"No, nothing was taken," said Sammy. "That's the strange part. According to Mr. Brenner, the twin vases were displayed openly on the kitchen table."

As the boys stepped out into the bright daylight, Brian closed the shop door. "But why break in if you're not going to steal anything?"

"Exactly," answered Sammy. "Why break in and then leave behind vases worth ten thousand dollars?"

The half-hour bike ride from Bird-in-Hand to Leola gave Sammy time to rethink the bizarre events of the day before. First, there was the aggressive bidding for what appeared to be two pieces of junk. And the two men bidding against Mr. Brenner were certainly odd. The small man in the back looked frail and homeless. And Sammy couldn't forget the man with the dark, thick glasses and white cane. It was that strange smile that Sammy found fascinating. Why would a man, who stopped bidding on something he apparently wanted, suddenly smile? Unless the man was trying to increase the bidding so Mr. Brenner would have to pay a higher price for the two items. But why do that? Sammy suspected there was something else behind the smile.

Sammy was also convinced that if anyone was trying to break into Mr. Brenner's green station wagon, it was the thin man. While the teenage detective made it a point never to accuse anyone without proof, the frail man seemed the only candidate. A blind man couldn't see well enough to quickly break into a car and then rummage around to find the vase.

But that smile?

Maybe Mr. Thick Glasses thought, Why bid on the vase? I can get it later for nothing. Sammy smiled. He liked that idea. But how . . .? Maybe Mr. Thick Glasses had a helper. Sure, the woman, wearing a lot of makeup, sitting beside him at the auction. She could do the dirty work for him. No.

Sammy's smile vanished. He had trouble imagining the woman breaking into the car and when that failed, breaking into Mr. Brenner's house.

But nothing was taken.

"Is that the place?" asked Brian over his shoulder, interrupting Sammy's train of thought.

Sammy saw the "Antiques For Sale" sign on the house. Paul Brenner's name was listed below as the proprietor. He nodded his head and followed Brian up the driveway.

Since Brian couldn't keep up with his friend intellectually, he always made an attempt to do so physically. So it was no surprise to Sammy when Brian produced an extra burst of speed that allowed him to arrive at the house first. In fact, Brian had his bike leaning against the porch and was displaying a big smile as Sammy arrived.

Paul Brenner stood at the back door of the old, two-story, brick building. "Come in this way, boys." He pointed to the door. "Here you can see where a crowbar was used to jimmy the door."

The splintered wood around the door knob and jamb showed how the intruder had entered the house. Traces of fingerprint powder showed that the police had been there also.

Sammy didn't notice anything unusual about the method of entry. "Did the police find any evidence?" he asked as he and Brian followed Mr. Brenner into a large kitchen. The teen detective recognized the three carton boxes on the floor with some of their contents scattered about. Drawers were pulled out, cabinet doors opened. On the kitchen table sat the two vases.

"The police tried to get prints. That's about it," said Paul, moving away from the boys. "Mary, come to the kitchen. Sammy and Brian are here."

The woman who entered the kitchen was different from what Sammy had expected. Mary was petite, five feet, three inches, quite a contrast to her burly, relaxed-dressed husband. She wore designer jeans and a striped, sleeveless blouse. Her brown hair was short and prim like the rest of her. But her brown eyes were sad as though part of her life had been sapped away.

Sammy saw that Mary Brenner was still shaken from the experience. He reflected back to the night of the break-in of his parents' store. It was Brian's and his first case, The Quilted Message. An intruder had entered through a window and tried to steal the album quilt. It's a strange feeling, knowing that someone has invaded your private world, knowing that someone has searched drawers, touched personal things. Even though nothing was taken, the idea of a stranger being there at night when you were asleep could cause anyone to feel violated.

"Mary, these are the boys from Bird-in-Hand who want to help us," said Paul. "They're very good at solving mysteries."

"Yes, Sammy and Brian. I've read about you in the newspapers," said Mary. "Well, we certainly have a mystery here. Don't we?" She walked to the table and allowed her fingers to slide down over the twin vases.

"And what mystery is that?" Brian wanted to know. He wasn't sure what Mrs. Brenner had in mind.

"These twin vases are the most expensive items we have in the house. Why didn't the prowler take them?"

The obvious answer to that, thought Sammy, was the intruder didn't know their value and was probably after something else. "Are you sure nothing was taken?" he asked.

"Nothing is missing from the rest of the house," replied Paul. "Everything I bought at the auction is right here in the kitchen."

Sammy made a quick survey. Part of him sensed that something was wrong. Then it clicked. Something was missing. He glanced up at Mr. Brenner.

"Where's the painting of the domino game?"

CHAPTER FOUR

Paul Brenner was dumbfounded for a second as if searching for the answer. His eyebrows raised, forming wrinkles across his forehead. He seemed surprised that the young detective would even mention it. He then laughed and shrugged. "Oh, the picture. I threw it away."

"When did you throw it away?" asked Sammy.

"Yesterday, right after I got home and showed it to Mary." He shook his head. "It's not worth anything. It's out in the trash."

No one said a word. They just glanced at each other.

They all had the same thought, but it was Mr. Brenner who spoke first. "Oh, my gosh. Do you think that's what the guy wanted?"

"But it's junk," said Mary. "I'm the one who told my husband to throw it out."

"Art is in the eye of the beholder," said Brian, trying to add culture to the conversation.

Sammy looked at his friend. "I think the original saying is, 'Beauty is in the eye of the beholder.'"

"Well, what I said is original. It's original with me," said Brian, producing his usual corny smile.

Paul Brenner moved toward the door. "Maybe I better go out and see if the painting is still there. I'll be right back."

As Paul reentered the house, he slipped the cardboard backing back under the nails and straightened the frame. "Here it is. I searched the back of it. There's nothing there worth stealing," he said and placed the painting faceup on the table.

The painting showed a close-up view of two men playing dominoes. Other lines and dabs of color suggested that one man was wearing glasses. One lens was black, the other pink. The other man had his back to the viewer.

"It's worthless. Why would anyone want it?" asked Mary.

"I must say my wife knows art," said Paul. "And if she says it's worthless, then it's junk. I don't think this is what the prowler was after."

Sammy wasn't so sure. He started to formulate a plan. "Do you mind if Brian and I take the picture with us?"

Paul pushed the painting towards Sammy. "No, you may have it. I'd just throw it out again."

As Sammy took the painting from the table, he completed his plan of action. It was a simple plan. One that would supply some needed answers.

He gave Mr. Brenner a serious look. "If anyone comes asking for this painting, wanting to buy it, tell them you gave it to us. Tell them that Sammy and Brian will have a table at Root's Country Market in Manheim. The painting will be for sale there on Tuesday."

"I think you're going to a lot of trouble for nothing," said Mr. Brenner. "However, if anybody shows up, I'll give you a call."

"Thanks," said Sammy. He glanced at Mary Brenner. "Brian and I would like to come back sometime to learn about those vases."

"Oh, yes, come back when all of this is over, and I'll show you my complete collection. Right now we have to get the house back in order. What a mess!"

As Sammy took one last look at the vases, he had a thought. "Mrs. Brenner, are you sure these vases are the same ones you left on the table last night?"

The color drained from Mary's face. In the excitement of the break-in, it never occurred to her to closely examine the vases. She assumed they were her vases. She picked up each vase, one at a time. Only she knew what to look for. After a few seconds, she expelled a sigh of relief and smiled. "Yes, these are my babies—my twins."

Sammy's bedroom, on the second floor of the old house, was the headquarters of the teenage detective team. The online computer sat silently but ready on the old oak desk. Books filled the wall-to-wall shelves opposite the window that overlooked Main Street. The wall behind the bed held plaques of various puzzle and mind-solving awards Sammy had won. Sammy's mother had insisted on the bulletin board that was next to the window. Sammy had suggested that the news items about their successful crime-fighting exploits could fit well in a bureau drawer. But Mrs. Wilson thought otherwise. And so a large cork board held the reports of Sammy and Brian's detective work. Of course, Sammy's mom had her copies of the articles neatly tucked away in an album.

Pieces of Sidney's disassembled painting lay on the desk. Stamped in small letters on the cardboard backing were the words: Framed in the wood shop at Fulton Prison.

Sammy leaned back in his chair, looked up at Brian who stood in front of the desk, and shook his head. "I would guess Sidney Thomas was an inmate of Fulton Prison when he painted this. I don't see anything in this painting worth fighting over. Do you?"

Brian smiled. "I could do a better painting than that. And what's this about our selling the painting at Root's Country Market?"

"Well, if someone is after the painting, let's give that person a chance to get it."

Brian's face lit up. "And then we'll know who it is. Right, Sammy?"

With chin in hand, Sammy bent forward and rested an elbow on the desk. He glanced again at the painting itself. "There's something odd about the painting though," he said. "Did you ever hear of a domino game where all of the dominoes are double sixes?"

Brian examined the painting again. "Hey, yeah, all the dominoes are double sixes. That's dumb. A regular set of dominoes shows dots from one to six. Heck, they even have sets now that are double nines, double twelves, and double fifteens. Who knows where it will end?" He frowned and shrugged. "Maybe he liked painting groups of six dots."

Sammy pinched his lips together and shook his head. "Or maybe he only had one domino as a model, and that was the double six."

Brian looked at his friend, not knowing whether Sammy was serious or was joking. The smile spelled it out for Brian. "Ha, ha, very funny," he said.

"Come on," said Sammy as he pushed himself away from the desk and stood. "Instead of sitting here guessing, let's go see Detective Phillips. He can run a check on this Sidney Thomas. I think that's where the answer is to this whole mystery. We should find out about Mr. Thomas and his connection to Fulton Prison."

The six-foot-two-inch, two-hundred-twenty-pound man smiled. The receding hairline, thin mustache, and penetrating eyes belonged to Detective Ben Phillips. The head detective of the local police department was always glad to see Bird-in-Hand's aspiring detectives. They made his job easier.

His office was small and cramped, and the two folding chairs weren't the most comfortable. If you sat sideways, your knees wouldn't press against Detective Phillips's desk. Take away the filing cabinet and the coffee cart and the office would be nine feet square. But you can't have an office without a filing cabinet and coffee maker.

After Sammy and Brian had settled in, the detective wanted to hear about their new mystery. Detective Phillips was always there for the youthful detectives. When they needed information, he usually supplied it. When they required backup, he provided it. When they wanted to set up a sting, he would supply the men. Their record as amateur sleuths was outstanding, but he did worry about their safety. That's why he tried to be included in their cases.

Detective Phillips grabbed a pen and slid a yellow tablet to the middle of his desk. "What's up?"

"Can you do a search on a Sidney Thomas?" asked Sammy. "He might have something to do with Fulton Prison."

The detective looked at the boys in surprise and dropped the pen on the desk. "I don't have to do a search. I already know about him."

Brian leaned forward in his chair. "Well, great. What can you tell us?"

The detective leaned forward also to meet Brian eye to eye. "He's dead."

Brian quickly retreated back from the powerful effects of Phillips's eyes and the dramatic disclosure of his words.

Sammy thought back to the afternoon of the auction. When Sidney Thomas's name was mentioned by the auctioneer, it created a minor stir. Evidently others had known this would-be artist named Sidney Thomas. "Did he die of old age?" he asked.

Detective Phillips smiled. "No, he died from a spoon."

"A spoon?" asked Brian.

"Yeah, one that was filed and shaped into a sharp knife."

"Are you saying he was stabbed in prison and died?" asked Sammy, picking up the clues in Detective Phillips's words.

The large detective rose, sat on the edge of the desk, and looked down at the teenagers. "That's exactly what happened. What are you boys into? Why do you want to know about Sidney Thomas?"

Sammy told Ben Phillips about the auction, the painting, Paul Brenner, bidders number 101 and number 28, and the break-in.

"Hey, Marvin, you over there?" yelled the detective, causing both boys to sit up straight in their chairs.

"Yeah. What do you want?" came a voice from the next office.

"You worked the break-in in Leola this morning, didn't you?"

"Yeah. But nothing was taken, and there were no prints," added Detective Marvin Wetzel as he leaned in through the open doorway. He saw the teenagers and smiled. "I see Sammy and Brian are here. They still doing your job for you?" he kidded.

"No," said Phillips, "this time they're doing your job. Call Conestoga Auction and find out who bidders number 101 and 28 were. Tell them it has to do with the break-in last night. Oh, also find out who owned the painting and the vase that were sold together yesterday." Phillips pointed a finger back over Marvin's head. "You can go back to your cage now. It's feeding time."

Marvin turned away, making animal sounds.

"Why was Mr. Thomas in jail?" asked Sammy. "Do you know?"

"Don't you boys remember the jewel robbery in Lancaster over a year ago? Someone squirted ketchup into a guy's face and grabbed a briefcase full of diamonds. The Lancaster police caught up with Sidney at Root's Country Market and Auction."

"Yeah, without the diamonds," said Sammy in recognition.

Brian nodded, "So that was Sidney Thomas who did the job."

"That was Sidney," repeated Phillips. "And . . . he had a partner who was never caught or identified."

"And the diamonds have never been found?" asked Brian.

"From what I understand, that's why Sidney was killed. Inmates tortured him, trying to get him to tell where he hid the diamonds."

"You think the diamonds are still somewhere at Root's?" asked Sammy.

"Unless someone has found them, and we don't know about it."

"But if the diamonds had been found, wouldn't they show up at a pawn shop or a fence somewhere?" asked Sammy.

Phillips smiled. "Not if someone recut them and made them into pieces of jewelry."

Brian's ears perked up. He took a deep breath, leaned back, and intertwined his fingers behind his head. "You mean they could be recycled."

Sammy rolled his eyes.

"That's exactly what could have happened," said Phillips.

"You said Sidney Thomas had a partner," said Sammy. "Couldn't he have the diamonds?"

The detective rose and squeezed his way to the window. He wanted to escape the limits of his small office. Now his eyes had room to wander over the countryside. One of the few benefits of his small office was the view. The police station fronted the Old Philadelphia Pike, Route 340. Farmland abounded for miles on both sides of the road. It was not uncommon for Detective Ben Phillips to be writing up a report and at the same time to be enjoying an Amish horse and buggy as it clippity-clopped by.

"As I recall," said Phillips, "Sidney's partner did the ketchup routine while Sidney grabbed the diamonds. Then they left the scene in two different cars. For some reason, Sidney headed for Root's where he was captured, minus the diamonds. They never did find or identify his partner." Phillips looked back at the teenage detectives. "The Lancaster detectives don't know if Sidney was able to pass the diamonds' location on to his partner."

"Sidney was arrested and put into jail," said Sammy. "His partner, not wanting to reveal himself, probably stayed away. So chances are, only Sidney Thomas knew where the diamonds were."

Brian tapped Sammy's shoulder. "He figured he'd pay the jail time then come out and recover the loot. Right, Sammy?"

Ben Phillips returned and stood at his desk. "Look, the reason I know about Sidney Thomas is that a good friend of mine is a Lancaster detective who's handling the case. Let me get in touch with him and I'll get you the up-to-date information on the diamonds. And, if you think it's important, I can call the warden at the prison."

"Yes, that's great. Thank you," said Sammy. He nudged Brian and stood.

"I'll give you a call later," said Phillips. "Will you be home?"

Sammy, deep in thought, nodded and headed for the door with Brian following. The diamonds were uppermost in his mind. He added them to the other ingredients in the developing case. Ah, he thought as he smacked his lips, this case is becoming more appetizing.

Did the painting have a connection to the diamonds? Sammy wondered. Was the painting the target of the break-in? Or was the intruder after money? Since the painting wasn't in Paul Brenner's house at the time of the break-in, Sammy couldn't be sure just what the prowler was after. He couldn't prove whether the bidders at the auction really wanted the painting or the vase.

After the boys left, Detective Ben Phillips returned to the window and watched as they mounted their bikes and pedaled off. He thought about Sidney's tragic, untimely death and about what the amateur detectives had told him. He shook his head and said aloud, "Boys, what have you gotten yourselves into this time?"

CHAPTER FIVE

Brian backed up to the bed and allowed himself to fall back. By the time the bouncing stopped, his eyes were focused on the ceiling. Sammy, settled in behind his oak desk, drew a tablet and pen from the drawer, and was ready to start the brainstorming.

Before he had a chance to throw out the first question, Brian spoke. "You know what I think we should do? After we set up our stand at Root's Country Market on Tuesday, we should take a walk around. Maybe we can find places where Sidney might have hidden the briefcase of diamonds."

"I'm sure the police have already done that many times," said Sammy. "Who knows how many other people have searched those buildings inside and out."

"So maybe somebody already found the diamonds. Right, Sammy?"

"Could be," replied Sammy. "Most people, though, if they found the diamonds, would turn them in and collect a reward. That way they get money without a guilty conscience." He shook his head. "But there's always that one person who keeps the gems and lives with the guilt."

"I was thinking about that," said Brian. "I might even be tempted to keep them."

"Really?" said Sammy, surprised at his friend's remark.

Brian sprang up on the bed. "Oh, don't get me wrong. I would be tempted, but I would return the diamonds."

Sammy was relieved to hear Brian say that. Then Sammy remembered something he had learned at school. Now was the time to make his friend aware of it. "A value isn't a value until it's acted upon," he said. "We all think we would always do the right thing. But, when we are faced with real life, it might be a different story."

Brian got defensive. "Well, I know if I found the diamonds, I wouldn't keep them."

Sammy's interest in human behavior had taught him, you never assume anything. He wanted to slip Brian that bit of wisdom but changed his mind. Brian, who after having cleared up the matter of his honesty, was back concentrating on the ceiling.

"Brian, let's start thinking like Sidney Thomas. You're in jail. You know where you hid the diamonds. Your partner is on the outside. What do you do? Do you try to contact your partner?"

"Well, I wouldn't tell my partner where the diamonds were. That's for sure," replied Brian.

"You think he might grab the diamonds and run."

Brian lifted his head from the bed. "You know what they say, 'There's no honor among thieves.'"

Sammy pictured the "spoon" that had ended Sidney Thomas's life. There's no honor among inmates in jail, he thought to himself. "Brian, if your life has been threatened by another inmate, and there's a chance you could die, would you reveal to your partner where the diamonds were?"

"Yeah, I might," answered Brian.

"Okay, now how do you get word out to your partner? He won't come to the jail. He doesn't want to be associated with you because he's afraid of the police. You can't write him a letter because it could be read by the police. So what do you do? How do you sneak it out without—"

"Oh, I see what you're getting at," said Brian. "Mr. Thomas suddenly develops an interest in painting. He paints a simple picture and frames it. But before he fastens the back to the picture, he slips in the directions to the diamonds. The police won't discover it because they don't know it's there. Right, Sammy?"

Sammy glanced down at the painting on the desk. "If that's what happened, then somebody got to the letter before the painting ended up at the auction."

"So you're saying that when we discover who brought the painting to the auction to sell, we might find the person who has the diamonds."

"It's worth investigating."

"But why all the interest in the painting at the auction?" asked Brian.

"There could be two answers to that, Brian. Either the bidders didn't know someone had already found the letter or . . . maybe it was the vase they were after."

"It has to be the painting because the vases weren't stolen at Mr. Brenner's house," added Brian.

"Maybe the intruder was after money," said Sammy, trying to keep the ideas flowing. "He found no money so he left."

Brian couldn't think of a reply so he said, "I like your idea of us displaying Sidney's painting at Root's. We let people know that we have the painting and then see if anyone comes after it. That way we'll know for sure if it's the painting they're after."

Sammy glanced at the picture. "You know what else is strange?" he asked. "That this painting showed up at the Conestoga Auction. It showed up at an auction house that just happens to be across the road from Root's Country Market, where the diamonds disappeared."

"Yeah, that is odd," said Brian, visualizing the two businesses that attract thousands of people each year.

"And, here's something even more mysterious," said Sammy. "If the painting had been used to find the diamonds, why would the person then send the worthless painting to an auction to be sold?"

These and other questions along with possible theories were discussed over the next hour. But the brainstorming came to an end with a thumping knock at the bedroom door.

"Open up. Let us in," came a booming voice, followed by more rapid pounding.

As Sammy was trying to analyze the situation, Brian sprang up to his feet and stammered, "Who . . . Who . . . Who is it?"

"Open up. It's the police."

CHAPTER SIX

From his desk, Sammy motioned for Brian to stay where he was. He leaned back, placed his hands behind his head, and took a deep breath. "You're going to have to wait until we're done," said Sammy.

Of all the dumb things to say, thought Brian, who at the time was preparing to disappear under the bed. "What are you doing?" he whispered to his friend.

Sammy's upraised hand told Brian to remain still and quiet.

"What do you mean we have to wait?" asked a thunderous voice.

"It's our tea time," replied Sammy, "and we haven't finished our cookies yet."

At that reply, the knob turned and the door sprang open. A tall, heavy-set man stepped into the room, his piercing eyes surveyed the area. He had something in his hand which he raised as he approached Sammy.

Sammy smiled.

The man smiled.

Brian had to go to the bathroom.

"I couldn't fool you, could I?" said Detective Ben Phillips, handing the folder to Sammy.

Sammy took the folder and glanced at Brian. "He couldn't fool us. Right, Brian?"

Brian's brow wrinkled. "I'll be right back. I have to go to the bathroom."

The papers inside the folder had Sammy's attention. He took his time and read through some of them while Phillips stood behind the teenager's chair and waited.

Brian returned and shot Phillips a pathetic look.

"It was time for me to go off duty," said the detective, "so instead of calling you with the information, I decided to drop by. Sammy, I stopped at your parents' shop next door looking for you boys, and your father suggested I come up here and do the police routine."

Brian took a deep breath. "And I guess if he told you to jump off a cliff, you would have done that, too!" he said, imitating all the parents who say that to their children.

Phillips smiled. "As a matter of fact, I liked the idea. I haven't pounded on any doors lately, and I need to keep in practice."

Before Brian could reply, Sammy said, "Brian, our numbers now have names. Number 101 is Nick Palmer. Number 28 is Benny Hayes."

Ben Phillips leaned over and pulled a sheet from the folder. "According to Jeff DeHart at the Conestoga Auction, this was Nick Palmer's first time there. Here you can see he did jail time for minor offenses."

"House break-ins?" asked Sammy.

Phillips nodded. "That's right up his alley."

"Any link to Sidney Thomas?" asked Sammy.

The detective shook his head. "None that I could find."

"What about Benny Hayes, our 'blind man'?" asked Sammy, looking for the paper that might have that information.

Brian came around the desk and stood near Sammy. "You shouldn't say blind. You should say visually impaired."

Ignoring his partner's comment, Sammy looked up at Phillips for an answer to his question.

"I kept the best for last," said the detective. "Sidney Thomas was an inmate in Fulton Prison all right, and guess who his cell mate was?"

Sammy pointed to the painting. "Benny Hayes. I bet that's him in the picture."

"Bingo," said Phillips.

A connection now existed between the blind man, Sidney Thomas, and the painting. Sammy came to the conclusion that the puzzle pieces were now worth putting together. He couldn't sit back and admire the puzzle just yet. The picture was incomplete. Phillips had certainly provided him with some answers, but he needed more. He would have to use the painting as bait to get more pieces of the puzzle.

"I talked to the warden, and he told me all about Benny," said Phillips. He walked around to the front of the desk to face the boys. "This you will not believe. Benny is a bank robber."

"So Benny Hayes can see," said Brian. "He really isn't blind."

"Oh, he's legally blind," said the detective.

Brian wasn't ready to believe what he was hearing. "Hey, are you trying to tell us that when you're dead you're dead, but when you're blind you can see?"

Phillips smiled. "According to the warden, Benny has an incurable eye disease. He's blind in one eye, and the other eye is deteriorating."

"How could he rob banks in that condition?" asked Brian.

"That's the amazing part. Listen to this. Benny takes a cab to the bank. He tells the cabby to wait while he makes a withdrawal. He focuses on a person's back and follows the form to the teller's window. When it's his turn, he slips the teller a plastic bag and a note which says, 'Put all your money in this bag and be quick. I have a gun.' He then takes the filled bag, sets his white cane in motion, and heads back to the door. He exits the bank, climbs into the waiting cab, and goes to the airport. Several hours later he's in Chicago where he deposits the money in a bank under an assumed name."

The boys shook their heads in disbelief.

"How many banks has he robbed?" asked Sammy.

"Five or six. He's spent half his adult life in jail. According to the warden, he's known as Blind Benny the Bank Bandit. Try saying that fast five times."

Brian's lips started moving. They stopped. They started again. They stopped. He frowned.

"Do you want to say it out loud?" asked Phillips, who saw Brian struggling over the words.

"Sure, it's easy. Blind Benny the Bank Bandit. Blind Blenny the Blank Bandit. Blind Benny the Blank Blandit. Blind Blenny the Blank Blandit. Blind . . . Benny . . . the . . . Bank . . . Bandit. See, it's easy. The trick is to keep your mind focused."

"Sounds like he's a very cunning man," said Sammy, wanting to get back on track.

"Don't let his handicap fool you," said Phillips. "He can be very dangerous. Be very careful. In fact, I'm going to insist that you keep me informed if you intend to confront him."

"Do you know what I was thinking?" said Brian. "Benny and Sidney were friends in prison. Sidney gets killed. So when Benny gets out of prison, he wants to buy the painting to remember his friend by. Right, Sammy?"

"There's another side to that," said Sammy, picking up the painting from the desk. "Since Benny Hayes was Sidney Thomas's cell mate, he definitely knows about the diamonds. He may have suspected the painting revealed the diamonds' resting place."

Phillips hurried around the desk. "So this is the painting that all the fuss is about."

Sammy held it at an angle so Detective Phillips had a better view. "This is it."

The detective made a face. "Not much to look at, is it? Hey, all the—"

"The dominoes are double sixes," interrupted Brian, wanting Phillips to know they had already made that discovery.

"Where do you boys go from here?" asked Phillips.

Sammy laid out their plan for renting a table and displaying the painting at Root's Market. "We're going to dangle the painting out in the open and see if anyone takes the bait."

"While I'm at Root's," said Brian, "I might take a walk and keep my eyes open for the diamonds."

Phillips shook his head. "Brian, I'm afraid those diamonds are long gone by now. That's my theory anyhow."

Brian pouted, but he wasn't ready to buy that idea. Not yet. He knew that when he concentrated and released his powerful, diamond-finder mental rays, they would pinpoint the exact location of the hidden diamonds. Yes, it was only a matter of time before Secret Agent Brian Helm would find and turn over the stolen diamonds.

Another case solved by little, old Brian Helm, boy detective, idolized by many, a model for all to—

"Brian, why do you have that dreamy smile on your face?" asked Sammy.

Brian muttered something and turned away.

"Oh, and one more bit of information," said Phillips as he took the folder back from Sammy and read from his notes. "The painting and vase belonged to Cheryl Zeiders. She's the one who sold them at the auction. She's a private, registered nurse. On Tuesdays she sells collectibles at Root's, building number nine.

The mystery of how Sidney's painting got to the auction was now solved, but that only created another mystery. Who is this Cheryl Zeiders? wondered Sammy, and where did she get the painting? Did she have a connection to Sidney Thomas?

"So Cheryl Zeiders is in building number nine," said Brian, raising his arms. "This case is getting to be the number game. Number 101, number 54, number 28, double sixes, and now number nine."

"Speaking of numbers," said Phillips as he looked at his watch and headed for the door, "I have to get home or my wife will do a number on me."

"Thanks for the information," yelled Sammy at the closing door.

Phillips shouted back, "Just be careful. Benny Hayes is a treacherous man." His heavy footsteps descending the stairs accented the warning.

Sammy picked up the painting. "Brian, when you look at this picture, what do you see?"

"Two men playing a game of dominoes."

"What's the next thing you notice?"

"A bunch of sixes," answered Brian.

Sammy's face developed a quizzical look. "Detective Phillips said Cheryl Zeiders was in building nine. The dominoes are all sixes. I wonder what we'll find in building number six?"

CHAPTER SEVEN

Acording to a map Sammy's mother had, building number six at Root's was a single cinder-block structure located near building nine. Sammy remembered the building as having hardware, crafts, and sports cards. He made a note to check it out on Tuesday.

Sammy's other suspicion had been correct. Paul Brenner called the next day and reported that two people had showed up at his house at different times, inquiring about the painting. One person was an attractive middle-aged woman with heavy make-up. According to Brenner, she had a New York accent and smelled of alcohol. The other person, a man in his forties, was thin and had deep creases in his face. As instructed, Paul informed both parties that Sammy Wilson and Brian Helm were now in possession of the painting. It would be available at Root's on Tuesday.

It wasn't hard for Sammy to match the description of the two people to the ones at the auction. Nick Palmer, number 101, was thin with a wrinkled face. A middle-aged woman, heavy on make-up, had sat next to Benny Hayes, the blind man. It made sense. Benny would need transportation since his physical handicap kept him from driving. The woman might be his wife or girlfriend.

♦ ♦ ♦ ♦

Tuesday couldn't come soon enough for Bird-in-Hand's amateur detectives. Officially, Root's opened at nine o'clock, but at eight-thirty the market was already alive with venders and shoppers. Cars filled a good portion of the parking areas devoted to Root's Country Market in Manheim. The auction on Root's side of the road was involved with goods grown on the farm—produce and poultry. The Conestoga Auction across the road dealt with just about everything else.

Most of the stands at Root's Country Market were located in nine buildings. Many of these buildings were connected, causing the shoppers to meander up one aisle and down the next, with a right turn here and a left turn there. Only the "regulars" knew where they were at any given moment.

Some stands hugged the outside walls of the structures. The rest filled in the open gaps between the buildings, leaving room for the shoppers to stroll, to buy, and to socialize. Many outside stands were under trees or had canvas or plastic roofs for protection from the sun and the rain.

Sammy and Brian's stand had no covering. It was just a plain eight-foot table, located outside building number one. Sammy had called Tom Longenecker, the manager of Root's Country Market, and had made arrangements to rent the space.

The boys helped Mr. Wilson unload the car. When Sammy had explained his plan to his parents, they suggested he sell Amish-made wall hangings, pillow covers, and aprons at the market. Since they needed something besides the painting to display, Sammy agreed to the idea. All the items were marked with price tags. Mrs. Wilson also gave the boys a cash box containing money to make change.

After they arranged the Amish cloth goods on the table, Mr. Wilson nailed a 2x4 stud standing up from the back of the table. It stood like a flag pole, but instead of a flag, it held Sidney's painting. Sammy had attached a wire to the frame so it could hang from a nail. It was his idea to make the painting noticeable, and at the same time, unreachable. On the second nail under the painting hung a sign, "Sammy and Brian's Amish Goods."

Sammy looked at the sign with its simple block printing. He realized that Brian and he had now committed themselves to whatever danger might lie ahead. The only way anyone was going to get at the painting was through them.

"Now remember," said Sammy to Brian after his father had gone, "we're looking for anyone who shows an unusual interest in the painting."

"I know. I know," replied Brian, who was sitting on a chair behind the table.

"And we have to keep our eyes on the painting," added Sammy. "There's no telling what somebody might do to get it."

"Aye, aye, Chief," said Brian, saluting.

Sammy ignored his friend's attempt at humor. He understood Brian's irritation. Nobody likes to be told what to do. He checked his watch. Almost nine o'clock. "Before it gets too busy, I'm going over to check out building six, and then I'll have a talk with Cheryl Zeiders in building nine. We need to know how she got Sidney's painting. I'll be right back." He was ready to give Brian more instructions, but he thought better of it. Instead he turned and headed for building six.

The super sleuth made a quick check inside and out of building six and found nothing suspicious. He tried to imagine a scared man in a hurry, trying to hide a satchel full of diamonds. Building six contained crafts, household items, tools, and sports cards. Sammy saw no cubbyholes or odd construction that could conceal the case. To make sure, he made another pass inside and out before heading next door.

Building nine was a flea market with a sign announcing jewelry, coins, and antiques. Actually the top floor boasted collectibles. Cheryl Zeiders's mass display was spread across the back of the room. Sammy had been there before when he avidly collected baseball cards. Now he was on a different mission.

Cheryl Zeiders had a smile for Sammy as she did for all her customers. She was in her early fifties, short and hefty, with salt and pepper hair. Cheryl was the grandmother type with a twinkle in her eye. Sammy wanted to learn what was behind that gleam.

"Hi, my name's Sammy Wilson. I was told that you were the person who had the domino painting for sale at the auction."

"Why is everyone so interested in that painting?" she asked, without losing the smile and sparkle in her eye.

"Who else was inquiring about it?" asked Sammy.

"Last Tuesday two men were here. One man was blind and had a woman with him."

"Ah," said Sammy, "and was the other man small, thin, about forty?"

Cheryl lost her smile and her eyes dimmed. "How did you know?"

"They were at the auction, bidding on the picture."

"Oh, so he made it," said Cheryl Zeiders. "I told the one guy if he wanted the painting, he had better hurry across the road to the auction."

"Yeah, well, he made it," said Sammy, remembering the man who hurried in and sat in the back.

"Who bought the silly painting? Do you know?"

"Paul Brenner. He's a—"

"Yeah, I know him. Antiques in Leola," said Cheryl, interrupting and nodding her head. "He's here today. I saw him earlier." She then added, "Do you remember how much the painting brought? I must wait two more weeks before I get my check."

"The painting along with a vase brought three hundred dollars," said the young detective.

Cheryl's mouth dropped open. "Three hundred dollars! Are you sure?"

"Yep, I was there," replied Sammy.

The bright smile and the twinkle returned. "Wow, I should send more of my slow-moving collectibles over to the auction."

Sammy didn't want to deflate her happiness. He decided not to tell her the true value of the vase. "Where did you get the painting?" asked the teenager, and he held his breath.

Cheryl hesitated as though searching for a way to explain. Or maybe she didn't want to reveal that information to anyone. She then took a hard look at Sammy and frowned. "Why are you asking all of these questions?"

Sammy knew she deserved the truth. He explained about Sidney Thomas, the diamonds, and how he and his friend, Brian Helm, believed the picture had something to do with the hidden gems.

When Sammy finished, he waited for a reply. He was not prepared for what he was about to see and hear.

The woman's face grew tense. Her body stiffened. With contempt in her voice she said, "Sidney Thomas was my stepbrother."

CHAPTER EIGHT

idney was your stepbrother?" repeated Sammy to make sure he heard correctly.

Cheryl turned away as two people approached and started to examine some Beanie Babies on display. Sammy followed Cheryl behind the counter. He needed to know much more.

"He was the black sheep in the family," she explained. "I wanted nothing to do with him. I told him that." She looked at Sammy. "He came here, you know. The day . . . the day he stole the diamonds. The police were after him. He wanted me to take the briefcase and hide it for him. When I refused, he got mad and hurried away."

"Did your stepbrother send you the painting from jail?" asked Sammy.

"I was his closest relative. After Sid was killed in prison, they sent me all his belongings. It wasn't much—the painting, a watch, rings. I sent it all to the auction." She shook her head. "Whatever made Sid believe that he could paint?"

Sammy brushed the hair from his eyes. "I believe it was the gems. Evidently, diamonds are not a man's best friend," he said. "Did you by any chance take the painting apart?"

"You mean take the back off?"

The super sleuth nodded.

"No."

"Ever receive any letters or notes of any kind that might tell where Sidney might have hidden the diamonds?"

"Sid wasn't the kind to write letters. I didn't touch the painting. I don't want anything to do with him. That's why I sent the stuff to the auction."

Sammy was watching for any signs of deceit. Had she found a note in her stepbrother's painting? Was this "grandmother" already sitting on a briefcase of diamonds? he wondered. Sammy raised his eyebrows. Brian had said even he might be tempted. The young detective looked again into Cheryl's eyes. She seemed truthful enough, but grandmothers were human, too.

"You'll have to excuse me. I have customers to wait on," said Cheryl as she glanced at the two women.

"Thank you for your time," said Sammy as he turned away. "Brian and I will let you know if we learn anything."

Cheryl Zeiders nodded. The smile and the twinkle returned. "If I can be of any more help, let me know," she called after the teenager.

The amateur detective headed for the side door, wondering whether the diamonds had caused that sparkle in Cheryl's eyes.

The small wooden deck beyond the door had a railing and ten steps that led down along the side of building number nine. When Sammy's foot hit the first step, he heard quarreling. He leaned over the banister and saw three people below, having a disagreement. He recognized the thick glasses and white cane.

It was them!

Benny Hayes, Nick Palmer, and the woman were standing by the stairs. Sammy noticed their position gave them a direct sight to Brian and the painting. He moved back away from the top step so as not to be seen. Cautiously, he leaned closer to hear their conversation.

"But you have no right to them. They're mine," came a thin, whiny voice.

"How can they be yours when you don't have them and probably never will?"

"Listen, Sid did that painting for me so I'd know where the diamonds were."

"Well, I shared that stinking cell with Sid for six months. I posed while he painted. He said if anything happened to him I could have his share."

The thin, shaky voice argued back, "Right from the beginning, we were all to get an even share. I was to get one-third of the loot."

"Well, I want in. I'm taking Sid's share. You still get your one-third."

"Boys, I think it would be better if you two work together," said a woman's voice coated with a New York accent. "Come on, let's go get the stupid painting."

Sammy didn't wait to hear more. He now had an important piece of the puzzle. It definitely was the painting they were after. Benny and Nick needed it to locate the diamonds. He went back inside and left by the front door. He maneuvered around the crowd to keep out of sight and hurried to be with Brian. The way it sounded, the trio would shortly be on their way over to get the painting.

Sammy slipped in behind the table next to Brian. "Don't ask questions and don't look," said Sammy, using a low, casual tone of voice. "Our friends are on the way over. Act natural."

Of course Brian had to see what he wasn't supposed to look at in order not to look at it. He held up an Amish apron and peered past its edge. He saw the threesome approaching. He couldn't miss the dark glasses and the white cane. The apron began to shake. Brian tried folding it but gave up and let it fall back onto the table. He looked at Sammy. "They're all together. They . . . they wouldn't harm us with all these people around. Right, Sammy?"

"Relax, Brian," said Sammy out the side of his mouth.

Brian's heart-beat rhythm went into double time as the enemy made a frontal attack.

Nick Palmer spoke first, his head tilted up. "How much is the painting?"

"I'm sorry," said Sammy quickly before Brian could speak, "but it's already sold."

"Sold? But it's up there on display," said Nick.

"We're holding it for someone. He's coming back later to pick it up."

"I'll give you a hundred dollars for it right now. No questions asked."

"I can't do that," said Sammy. "The painting is sold."

Nick reached over and grabbed Sammy's arm. "Look, you're not hearing me. I want that painting. If you don't . . ."

The woman stepped in. "Now, now, Nicky, calm down." She patted Nick's shoulder. "I know how much you wanted that painting, but we'll get you another one," she said as the pat turned into one big pinch. The heavily made-up face descended on the boys. "You see, Sidney Thomas, who painted the picture, was like a father to Nicky here. Sidney died recently and Nicky is in shock. He wanted the painting. It would be like having a part of Sidney back again."

Oh, brother, thought Sammy. The only thing missing were the tears. And good thing, too. With all that make-up, tears would have produced a lava flow down her face.

The crowd was heavier now. People moved slowly from stand to stand, inspecting the day's goodies. Three woman stopped to check out the Amish items. The older woman held an apron up in front of her daughter and said, "That's the one you should buy." Another woman leaned over the table and pointed to a cloth wall hanging. "Are these really made by the local Amish?" she asked.

Sammy glanced quickly at the woman and leveled his hand over the cloth merchandise. "Yes, it's all made by the Amish." His attention returned again to the trio. He shrugged. "As I said, the painting is sold. Sorry."

"Let's go," said Benny Hayes, tapping his cane against the woman's leg.

Brian stepped out from behind Sammy, looked at the woman who grabbed Benny's arm, and said, "How about an apron?"

"I don't do kitchen!" she snapped as the three turned and were soon swallowed up in the crowd.

"Well, we handled that all right. Didn't we?" said Brian, standing tall, pulling up his pants, and speaking in his secret agent voice.

"They'll be back. You can count on it," said Sammy, producing a blank stare.

Brian lost some height and his deep voice shot up two octaves. "They . . . they will?" he stammered as Sammy stepped aside to handle the customers.

After ten minutes of selling two aprons and a wall hanging, the boys looked up into the lens of a camera. It was within three feet and pointed directly at them. Sammy smiled. "Hey, Joyce," he said. "What are you doing here?"

Joyce Myers was Sammy and Brian's age. Her short-cut brown hair framed an oval face. Her large hazel eyes, which didn't miss much, peeped above her camera. "I'm doing a report about Root's Country Market," she answered, "and it looks like you're part of it today."

Sammy gave Joyce a long, hard look. "So you just happen to show up the same Tuesday that Brian and I are here."

"Okay, okay, so I heard you guys are working on a new case," admitted Joyce. "May I help?"

The bright, teenage girl had joined the Sammy and Brian detective team to solve other cases: Amish Justice, Doom Buggy, and Fright Train. She was extremely talented in critical thinking, writing, and photography. Joyce had her own darkroom and could develop and print her own black and white pictures. She was preparing to be a photojournalist.

"Sure, you may help us. Right, Sammy?" said Brian.

Sammy cleared some merchandise from a corner of the table. "It just so happens that we need some photos taken," he said. "Here, jump up on the table and take some shots of the buildings and the crowd. We may need them later."

"Wait till you hear about the diamonds," said Brian as he moved the chair closer for Joyce to step on.

From her new vantage point, Joyce could see over the heads of the crowd. She also came face to face with Sidney Thomas's painting hanging on the pole. She grimaced. "Hey, I have news for you guys.

This painting still isn't far enough away. I can still see it."

"That's a work of art," joked Brian. "Go into any art museum in the world and you can see stuff just like that."

After pivoting and snapping several shots, Joyce again confronted the painting. "The painter goofed. These dominoes are all—"

"Double sixes," said Brian. "Yeah, we know." He took a deep breath and smiled at Joyce.

"While you're standing there," said Sammy, "take a closeup of the painting. We may need that, too."

"Maybe we'll appreciate the painting better in black and white," joked Brian.

The zoom lens buzzed as Joyce focused in on the painting and took two shots.

When Joyce got down from the table, Brian took her aside and told her about the auction, Paul Brenner and the vase, the two men and woman, and Sidney and the diamond heist.

Pointing, Joyce asked, "If that painting doesn't contain the information about the diamonds, then why are people after it?"

Sammy, who was listening as he sold a cushion cover to a woman, said, "If there was a written message in that painting, someone already has it. We took the painting apart. There's nothing there." Sammy's eyes got larger and he raised his index finger. "However, Benny Hayes and Nick Palmer don't know that. They think the information is still there."

Brian gripped Sammy's arm. "If the painting has nothing to do with the diamonds, why didn't you sell the dumb thing to Nick for the hundred dollars he offered?"

Before Sammy could answer, a man interrupted. "Hi, you Sammy and Brian?"

"Yes, we are," answered Brian proudly.

"Detective Ben Phillips told me you'd be here."

"What can we do for you?" asked Sammy.

"I'm Fred Price. I'm the gem salesman who was robbed."

The man was sixty-four, of medium height and slightly overweight. His graying hair, pale skin, and dull eyes revealed the toll of spending a lifetime on the road, going from jewelry store to jewelry store, selling his gems.

Brian looked the man up and down and visualized him carrying a briefcase full of diamonds. "Did they really squirt ketchup on you?" asked Brian.

Fred Price frowned, nodded, and then pointed up to the painting. "Is that the picture that's suppose to tell where the diamonds are?"

"We're not sure, but several people think it does," said Sammy.

"So the briefcase hasn't been found yet," said Fred.

"Not that we know of," said Sammy, shaking his head. "But, didn't the insurance company reimburse your employer for the stolen diamonds?" he asked.

"Yes, after the investigation, they got the insurance money. Look, I'm going to retire soon. When I first got the job, my wife gave me the brief-case as a gift. She's dead now . . ." He took a deep breath. "It's a hard-shell, leather case. I'm not interested in the gems. It's just that I'd like to get my briefcase back, that's all. It means a lot to me."

"If we find it, we'll let you know," said Sammy.

Joyce stepped forward and extended her hand. "I'm Joyce Myers, a friend. Were you able to identify the two men who attacked you?"

Fred shook Joyce's hand as he replied. "No, the man who approached me from the front was hidden behind a grocery bag. After that, all I saw was the red slop coming at me."

"I guess the briefcase was locked," said Brian.

"No, it wasn't."

"You had a million dollars' worth of diamonds in the case, and it wasn't locked?" said Brian.

"With diamonds inside, how long do you think it would take a crook to split a steel case even if it was locked?" asked Fred Price. Not expect-ing an answer, he continued. "A lock is not going to deter anyone from getting at those diamonds. We don't carry the gems around in a strong box with locks all over it. You have to understand," said Fred, "we can't advertise that we're carrying valuable gems. Believe it or not, sometimes we carry the diamonds in a simple, canvas duffel bag."

"But wouldn't a serious jewel thief know what you look like?" asked Joyce.

"You should see some of the stuff I carry in my car to change my appearance. I have special clothing and hats. Usually glasses and a beard will do it. I don't set up an arrival time at any particular jewelry store. Even the store manager doesn't know when I'll show up."

Sammy started to realize the working conditions jewel merchants endured. He tried to visualize the robbery then said, "Do you think Sidney and his partner had the store staked out for days, waiting for you?"

Fred nodded. "They did a lot of research and had some luck thrown in with it."

"Do you have a card so we can keep in touch should your briefcase turn up?" asked Sammy.

Fred slipped a card from his pocket. With a pen he added a number. "I wrote my home telephone number."

"Ah, huh, another number," said Brian.

Sammy smiled and took the business card Fred handed him. He quickly scanned the information. "Oh, you have a Lancaster address, I see."

"Yes, the company I work for is in New York, but I work out of Lancaster," said Fred. "Lancaster County is part of the territory I cover." He glanced at his watch. "I have to go. Please keep in touch."

"We'll do that," replied Brian as Fred Price hurried toward the parking area.

"He seems like a nice guy," said Joyce. "I hope he gets his case back."

"I'll find it for him," said Brian, casting a glance at the painting to make sure it was still there.

Sammy wasn't listening to his friend. He was busy waiting on customers.

After several sales were made, the teenagers' eyes were immediately drawn to a crowd forming fifteen feet from the stand.

"Oh, the man fell down," came a voice nearby.

"Careful, he's blind," said another.

As Sammy, Brian, and Joyce joined the group, a familiar made-up face forced its way through the spectators. "Benny, I told you not to go on your own. You must stay with me," scolded the woman. She got the blind man to his feet and led him away.

"What was that all about?" asked Brian.

Sammy spun around. Finally, he swallowed hard and pointed. "That's what it's all about!"

The others looked up.

The painting was gone.

CHAPTER NINE

"**H**a, ha, the joke's on them," laughed Brian. "When they take the painting apart, they won't find anything."

Sammy didn't find the incident humorous. He couldn't believe he fell for a stunt like that. Benny and the woman had created a diversion, while Nick stole the painting. He had been tricked, and he didn't like it. Well, it was too late now. His only hope was that the painting would be worthless to them.

Joyce felt bad but knew Sammy would bounce back. "What's next?" she asked.

Sammy thought ahead. Now was the time to tell Brian and Joyce the conversation he had with Cheryl Zeiders and what he overheard outside building nine. He finished by saying Nick Palmer had been Sidney's partner in the robbery.

"But it can't be proven," said Joyce.

Sammy thought through all that had happened since the auction. His blue eyes projected the sadness and the hopelessness he felt. He shook his head. "I believe our case just dissolved. Actually, there never was a case. The diamonds are still missing. That's the important fact right now."

"Do you still want the pictures I took for you?" asked Joyce, holding up her camera for Sammy to see.

"Yeah. Bring them to the house when you have them printed."

"The only thing left for us to do is find the diamonds. Right, Sammy?"

"We need clues to do that," said Sammy. He held out his empty hands. "I don't see any here."

"How long are you guys going to be here today?" asked Joyce.

"My father's coming back at four."

Joyce backed up, took a quick picture of Sammy and Brian, turned, and waved. "See you guys later. I'm going to take some more pictures."

"And I'm hungry," said Brian, patting his stomach.

"Fink's French Fries is over there," said Sammy, pointing. Then he reversed himself. "Up this way is Hess's Barbecue. Just ask for Karen."

Brian squinted. "Do you think they sell hot dogs and sauerkraut here at Root's?"

"They probably do. They have just about everything here," said Sammy.

Brian frowned. "Yeah, even a million dollars in diamonds—somewhere. You know what I always say about Root's?"

"I'm afraid to ask," said Sammy.

Brian stuck his thumbs into his belt. "I always say, 'If you can't buy it at Root's, you shouldn't have it.'"

A woman who overheard Brian's remark held up a quilted pillow cover in front of the boys and grinned. "That's just the push I needed. I'll take this. It's here so I should have it."

Sammy took the money, put the merchandise into a plastic bag, and gave it to the woman. "Thank you," he said with a smile.

After the woman left, Brian coughed, tugged at his pants, and stretched. "See the power of words? I think I'll come up with some other sayings."

"Oh, Brian, get your hot dog," said Sammy, pushing his buddy away from the table. "And then, why don't you go looking for the diamonds?"

"Good idea," said Brian, heading for the door of building number one. "I even have a saying for that one, too. 'Never go searching for diamonds on an empty stomach. You never know what you'll eat when you're hungry.'"

Sammy watched his friend disappear into the building and then glanced up at the pole. He couldn't change what had happened. The painting was gone.

❖ ❖ ❖

Nicky ran with the painting in one hand and the white cane in the other. The nail, protruding at an angle from the end of the cane, made it easy to snatch up the painting from the pole. He headed for his car in the back parking lot. Benny and the woman would be waiting for him there. His pace changed from a slow run to a fast walk. No use drawing attention to himself.

Nick thought of his accidental meeting with Benny and the woman that morning. They were standing beside building nine, watching the boy detectives set up their stand. They recognized each other from the auction. An argument ensued, and with a little encouragement from the woman, they ended up working together with one goal in mind—getting the painting and finding the diamonds.

Well, now he had the painting, and—

The forced whisper filtered through the hooded mask. "Give me the painting, now." Those words and the appearance of a gun persuaded Nick to stop and give up the painting, fast.

Twenty feet away at the car, Benny and the woman were waiting for the arrival of Nick and the painting. Only the woman saw what was happening. She explained to Benny what was taking place. The masked man was running away with their painting.

Right inside building number one was Bev's Snack Bar. The first item listed on the wall menu was hot dogs, the second—hot dogs with sauerkraut. Brian smiled. This is going to be my lucky day, he thought as he placed his order.

Munching on his favorite sandwich, Brian ventured forth in his quest for the lost diamonds. Okay, now I'm Sidney Thomas, he thought to himself. I have a briefcase full of diamonds. What do I do? He glanced down the long aisle with stands on both sides. He read the signs—Fireside Crafts, Donegal Gardens Produce, Raub's Sub Shop, Hahn's Sea Food, Glick's Cheese, Aunt Bobbi's Fudge, Burkhart's Bakery, Richard M. Heagy Deli, Bird-in-Hand Bakery, Brenda's Flowers, Knepp's Caramel Corn, New Holland Meat Market, and Smith's Candy. Brian's senses were overloaded with goodies. How was he going to keep his mind on the diamonds?

Brian took a bite of the hot dog and concentrated real hard. I have to find a place not easily seen, thought the young detective. An out-of-the-way place. Yet it has to be a location that Sidney could get at easily and without being seen.

Brian slipped into his secret agent mode, double-oh-seven and a half. He stood tall. His face hardened. His eyes radiated the mystery and charm that drew hundreds of girls to his side. Too many, in fact. So he relaxed, allowing some of his charm to drain away. Two girls would be enough for the day. His left hand, holding the hot dog, became heavier as he extended his index finger. This was the special gun he used in emergencies. Only emergencies. He never really shot anyone yet, but he did poke out a lot of eyes.

His mental image softened as some sauerkraut and its juice dribbled down over his gun . . . ah, his left hand. A lady from behind nudged him to move forward. He was holding up the flow of traffic that traveled up and down the crowded aisles. He looked back at the woman. Doesn't she know he was about to find the long, lost, hidden diamonds? He sighed, took a bite out of the hot dog, and humbly trudged ahead with the crowd. He would have to go with the flow, accepting his image as a follower.

This is the same situation Sidney was in, thought Brian. He had to move with the people traffic, unless he stopped at a stand or exited from one of several doors. Brian decided to make the rounds of the buildings first before he ventured outside. He would move ahead with the group until he saw a possible hiding place just as Sidney might have done.

After traveling here and there, turning left and right, being pushed and shoved, Brian was lost. And, he hadn't found any cavities that could conceal the briefcase of diamonds. To add to his frustration, he had finished eating his hot dog somewhere along the journey, and now his fingers were sticky.

When Brian dug into his pocket for a tissue, his fingers felt something very small and hard with rough edges. He withdrew the object and examined it.

He couldn't believe what he held in his hand! It looked like a diamond!

CHAPTER TEN

Was the diamond real?

It seemed real to Brian. He glanced around as he closed his hand to hide his find. Then just as quickly, he opened his fingers to look again at the gem. It was still there. But how did it get into his pocket? Had he accidentally bumped against the hiding place and the diamond fell out? No, the diamonds were in the briefcase. Ah, wondered Brian, did Sidney spill the gems from the case in order to fit them into a smaller container? Would he have had time to do that? The police were right behind him. He would still have to get rid of the briefcase. Oh, this all doesn't make sense, he thought to himself.

The budding detective was excited and confused. He couldn't wait to get back to Sammy, but first he needed to know how to get out of this maze.

Down the aisle and to his right was the D & D Jewelry counter. Brian pinched the shiny gem between his thumb and index finger. I can kill two birds with one stone, he thought, smiling to himself at the pun. The jeweler can tell me if this diamond is real, and he can direct me to the nearest exit.

The jeweler saw the teenager approaching. The boy was smiling but had a strange look on his face. He was holding something very small in his hand. The teen pressed against the stand and held the sparkling stone before the jeweler.

Dan Hall, forty-seven, was six feet tall with thinning hair and a mustache. He took the diamond and examined it. "That's a nice stone. Where did you get it?"

"I . . . er . . ." The boy hesitated. He seemed bewildered. Finally he answered. "I found it in my pocket."

Dan Hall winced. Something wasn't right here.

"Is it real? How much is it worth?" the teen asked.

"What it's worth and what you can get for it are two different things," answered the jeweler, glancing again at the gem and then back at the boy. "Since you want to sell it, I'll have to go to my car to get the electronic diamond tester." Dan turned to his wife, standing nearby. "Here you hold this till I get back." He hurried around the counter and was soon gone.

The woman smiled. She was short, stocky with short auburn hair. "I'm, Beth, Dan's wife. He won't be long." She held up the gem. "This is a beautiful stone," she said, smiling, trying to put the boy at ease.

"But I don't want to sell it," said the boy. "I just want to know if it's real."

"My husband will be able to tell you when he comes back with the tester," said Beth Hall.

Minutes passed. Brian took a deep breath. How did I get into this mess? he wondered. He looked around. "Which way do I go to get out of this building?" he asked, thinking he'd save time by asking now.

But Beth didn't have time to answer. Her husband returned, carrying a small, hand-held, electronic diamond tester. Dan went behind the counter, took the stone from Beth, and carefully pressed the tester against the gem. "If the diamond is real," said Dan, "the waves moving through the stone will cause this green light to flash."

The light flashed green.

"It's genuine all right," said Dan Hall, smiling and holding the gem up for all to see. "You have a beautiful two-carat diamond here." He stared at Brian and lost the smile. "That's too large and valuable for a boy to just find in his pocket. Where did you really get this diamond?"

Brian started to stutter.

A policeman suddenly appeared from nowhere.

Now Brian couldn't talk at all, and he had to go to the bathroom, badly.

"Hi, I'm Sergeant Harold Gainer. Are you Dan Hall, the person who called?" he asked and stepped behind the counter.

"Yes, and this is the boy," said Dan. "Here's the diamond. It's real. I just tested it." He handed the stone to Sergeant Gainer.

The policeman stared down at the teen. "What's your name?"

"B . . . B . . . Brian Helm."

"Where did you get the diamond?"

"Look, I know it sounds dumb," replied the teen, "but about twenty minutes ago I put my hand in my pocket and . . . and there it was. In my pocket. It was just there. Even I couldn't believe it. It's one of those dumb things that happen."

"It's dumb, all right," said the Sergeant. "Are you aware that stolen diamonds disappeared here? They've never been found." He gave Brian another stern look. "Or have they? Did you find this diamond here at the market?"

Brian didn't know how to answer the policeman. He found the diamond in his pocket, and he was certainly here at the market. So technically he did find it here.

Before he could answer, Sergeant Gainer said the words Brian didn't want to hear. "You'll have to come with me to the station."

"But I didn't steal it, honest," said Brian. "You can call Detective Ben Phillips of the Bird-in-Hand police. He'll tell you. I'm Brian. My friend, Sammy Wilson and I . . . We're the amateur detectives from Bird-in-Hand. We help the police. We're working on a case now. You remember Sidney Thomas? He's the guy who hid the diamonds. Well, he painted a picture in prison, and . . . and . . ."

"Hoa, hoa, slow down," said the Sergeant. "So you know about Sidney Thomas. Are you saying that you found the diamonds?"

"Well, yes . . . no . . . I don't know."

"Okay, tell me again. Where did you get that diamond? And if you don't tell the truth this time, I'm taking you to the station."

Sammy sat behind his desk, his attention focused on Brian. His friend was sitting on the edge of the bed with his head tilted down. He was not smiling. He looked like a little boy who was caught with his hand in the cookie jar. A jar full of diamonds. Standing beside the desk was Detective Ben Phillips, holding a diamond in the palm of his hand.

"Brian, I vouched for your character and your honesty at the station. If no one reports a two-carat diamond lost or stolen within thirty days, it's yours. In the meantime, it stays with me."

The shallow smile Brian released was hardly worthy of a person about to "inherit" a diamond worth twenty to thirty thousand dollars. "I'd feel better about it if I thought you two believed me. But you don't, do you?"

The thought that kept running through Sammy's mind were the words Brian had spoken the day before: "I might be tempted to keep the diamonds." Sammy had to believe that his best friend did find the diamond in his pocket. He looked up at Phillips. "Thanks for what you did at the police station. For getting Brian out of trouble."

"He's not out of trouble yet. He's still under suspicion."

Brian threw himself back on the bed. "I can't believe they took me to the station and called my parents," he growled, trying to concentrate on the ceiling.

"Hey, this could be one of the stolen diamonds," said Phillips, shaking his hand. "You're right. I'm not sure I buy your story."

Brian lifted his head off the bed. "I put my hand in my pocket and there it was. That's it, Fort Pitt. That's all she wrote, Grandfather's goat."

"That sounds like a lie, Martha's pie," continued Phillips, showing Brian that he could play that game, too.

"Well, I believe Brian," said Sammy in a serious tone. "Now, let's go from there. Either someone put the diamond in Brian's pocket, or it fell in accidentally."

Phillips pointed to Brian's jeans. "Those pockets are pretty tight. No way did the diamond accidentally fall in."

"But why would someone give me a diamond?" asked Brian, his eyes still on the ceiling.

"By giving us one of the diamonds, maybe that person is trying to tell us that the diamonds have already been found," said Sammy, leaning back in his chair and placing his hands behind his head. He glanced up at Ben Phillips to get his reaction.

Phillips shrugged. "Hey, don't look at me, you're the brain here. I'm only a dumb cop. I have no idea why someone would give away diamonds."

Brian sprang up to a sitting position and focused on the detective.

"Why the silly grin on your face?" asked Phillips.

"I don't know if I want a dumb detective keeping my diamond for me," replied Brian.

"What diamond?" kidded Phillips.

"Yeah, right," said Brian, falling back on the bed again. "Remember, that diamond was put in my pocket, not yours."

Sammy brought the discussion back on track. "Now, why would someone want us to know the diamonds have been found?"

No one spoke.

Finally Brian answered the question. "So we don't waste our time trying to find them."

"Are you suggesting that someone is feeling so sorry for us that they gave away a two-carat diamond?" asked Sammy.

"What's a two-carat diamond to someone who has a million dollars' worth?" said Brian, trying to backup his statement.

Detective Phillips slid his hand back over his thinning hair. "Brian does have a point there. The person might think you'll find him and the diamonds if you keep looking. He's willing to give up a diamond to stop you."

Brian's head shot up from the bed. "Sure, he's buying us off. Don't you see? He wants us to stop our investigation."

"Speaking of investigation," said Sammy to Phillips, "I wanted to tell you I spoke to Cheryl Zeiders this morning. She told me that Sidney Thomas was her stepbrother."

"Now that's interesting," said Phillips. "That's why she had the painting and why Sidney ran to Root's Country Market with the police on his tail."

"According to her, she didn't help him," added Sammy.

Detective Phillips walked over to the bulletin board. "Cheryl Zeiders didn't want to end up in jail with her stepbrother," said Phillips. "That makes sense." His eyes fixed on several newspaper accounts of Sammy and Brian's exploits as amateur detectives. His name was usually included in the articles along with his picture. He was wondering whether this case would make the news. He didn't think so.

"Let's assume the diamonds have been found," said Sammy. "What's our next move?"

Phillips turned away from the articles. "Even if Sidney's painting was stolen from you boys today," said Phillips, "what good is it going to do anyone? The painting's worthless. You boys have no next move. It's in the hands of the Lancaster police." Ben Phillips raised his hands. "Sorry. With that piece of logic, I will leave you now." He opened and closed the door.

"Don't lose my diamond!" Brian yelled after him.

Words filtered back through the wall. "What diamond?" Then came the remains of a hearty laugh and the groan of the old stairway.

Brian's head rested back on the bed. His eyes reclaimed the ceiling. "Okay, so The Brief Case of the Missing Briefcase is over." Brian slid into his secret agent voice. "But I'm going to keep it open under the code name: The Number Game."

"Let's face it. It wasn't much of a case to begin with," said Sammy.

"The way I see it," said Brian, "we're at a dead end. That's all."

"Oh, no, you're not," came a voice from the other side of the door.

"Ah, we're being spied on," said Sammy, recognizing the voice.

"What kind of a detective would I be if I didn't listen at keyholes?" said Joyce Myers, opening the door. "I just passed Detective Phillips. What was he laughing about?"

"It's easy to laugh when you have thirty thousand dollars in your pocket," Brian answered.

Joyce looked to Sammy for the details, who explained that Phillips was holding the diamond until a decision was made as to its ownership.

"I heard about the diamond from your parents at the shop," said Joyce. "I thought I'd get to see it when I came up."

Brian was in no mood to talk about the diamond. "What did you mean by saying we're not at a dead end?" he asked. "What do you know that we don't know?"

"It's not what I know. It's what I have," said Joyce, waving a handful of photos. She placed the stack of twelve, black and white 8x10 photographs on the desk. On top were closeup copies of Sidney's painting. She selected one and said, "I thought about what you told me regarding Sidney and the diamonds. I think you're right about Sidney using the painting to get word out to his partner. The more I look at this painting, the more I believe it's the picture itself that contains the information."

Sammy picked up a photo and examined it. "Any ideas?"

Joyce frowned. "Double six is twelve. How about a building number twelve. Anything like that at Root's?"

"Nope, only goes to nine," said Sammy.

Joyce ran a finger from domino to domino. "The number six seems to be important. It's painted over and over. There must be a building number six at Root's."

"Yes, there is, and we already covered that," said Sammy. "I inspected building six twice today. I didn't find anything."

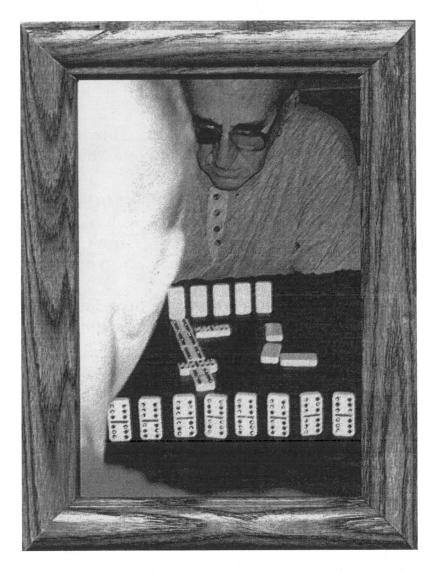

Joyce made a face and collapsed into the rocking chair. She glanced again at the photo. "The sixes dominate the painting. What else could they be telling us?" She wiggled and squirmed until the rocker cushions were molded to her body. She glanced at Brian. "Somebody's been sitting in my rocker," she pouted in a teasing way.

Brian waved his thumb at Sammy.

"Maybe Sidney had a fixation with sixes," said Sammy in desperation.

"I would guess he painted, using live models," said Joyce. "He had Benny and another man pose as he painted."

"They probably do play dominoes in jail," said Brian. "It helps pass the time."

Joyce tightened her eyes. "I can't picture a blind man playing dominoes. Do you think he did?"

"Sure, he could feel the indented dots," said Sammy. "When you're blind or near blind, your senses become more sensitive. Benny could identify each domino by feeling the number of dots."

"It's too bad Sidney Thomas, the artist, wasn't as sensitive and observant," said Joyce.

"Why, what do you mean?" asked Sammy.

"Well, look here." Joyce left the rocking chair and slid the enlargement on the desk in front of Sammy. "Since the dots are identical, each being a recessed dimple, they should all reflect highlights the same way. But look here. In the painting Sidney put a dab of white paint on only some of the black dots to indicate the reflected light. He only highlighted some of them."

Sammy made a quick inventory of the dabs of white specks and pictured Benny with the dominoes. "I must be slipping," he replied. "I should have noticed that before. I believe that's the message."

Brian pick up the third copy of the 8x10. "You mean those dots are going to tell us where the diamonds are hidden?"

"That's right," answered Joyce as she noticed the pattern laid out by the white specks of paint.

"It's like Morse code, dots and dashes. Right, Sammy," said Brian, studying the layout of the dots. "The black circles with white spots are the dots; the black circles without the highlights are dashes."

Sammy slid his chair over slightly to be in front of the computer. He soon had the monitor indicating that he was online and waiting for instructions. With a click of the mouse, he had a search engine ready to do his bidding. The teenage detective typed in one word. He waited for the results of the search. A list of responses downloaded from the web.

Sammy clicked number three.

After a ten-second wait, he had exactly what he wanted.

The smile on Sammy's face was all that Brian needed to know. His friends, Sammy and Joyce, had revived the case. They would soon be back on track and running. Brian glanced at the photo. The black dots stared back. What was the message that lingered among them? he wondered.

Sammy clicked the "print" button, made three copies, and handed one to each of his two partners. Joyce was now definitely part of the detective team.

Brian took one look at the printed material and said, "But this isn't the Morse code. It's braille."

"Which system of code would Sidney think of using, having a blind man as a cell mate?" asked Sammy.

"The braille system," answered Joyce.

Sammy reached into a drawer and handed them a pen and paper. "As you can see, the braille system is based on a pattern of six dots arranged as on a domino. So match up the highlighted dots on the painting with the larger black dots on the braille alphabet printout. Let's see what we each come up with."

After about five minutes, Sammy lifted his head and lowered his pen. "Well, have you figured out the pattern?"

A	B	C	D	E	F	G	H	I	J
K	L	M	N	O	P	Q	R	S	T
U	V	W	X	Y	Z	and	for	of	the
with	ch	gh	sh	th	wh	ed	er	ou	ow

"Yeah, you go across the top row of sixes then it continues across the bottom row," said Joyce.

Brian agreed, but he wasn't sure to what he was agreeing.

"What's the message you got?" asked Sammy.

"I separated the letters to read—block house on wall," said Joyce. "But I don't know about the dominoes that are lying flat on the table. They don't make sense."

"The dominoes with the message seem to be the ones standing up," said Sammy. "Since I got the same message, let's go with that."

"Could one of the stands at Root's have a house made of blocks hanging on a wall?" asked Joyce.

"I don't remember seeing one," said Sammy, "but one of the hobby stands might have a block house large enough to hold a briefcase." He wrote that possibility on his note pad.

"How about the outside area at Root's that has the wooden stuff?" asked Brian.

"You mean like gazebos and playhouses?" responded Joyce.

"Yeah, made of wood," said Brian.

"Wait a minute," said Sammy. He got up, went to the book shelf, and grabbed an encyclopedia. He searched through the B's. "Here it is, 'blockhouse.' Says here a blockhouse is a small fort built of wooden logs, part of a large defense system. It says early settlers built blockhouses to protect themselves from Indian attacks. They had small holes in the sides through which a rifle could be fired."

"There's nothing like that at Root's," said Brian.

"I'll be right back," said Sammy, and he disappeared for several minutes. When he returned he sported a smile. "If you people can be here at eight-thirty tomorrow morning, my father will take us to Root's. He said he can visit a friend in Manheim then pick us up on his way back. Meanwhile we can search for the house made of blocks."

"We'll be here," said Joyce and Brian in unison.

The three aspiring detectives' thoughts returned to the coded message. Finally Joyce asked, "How do you attach a briefcase with a million dollars' worth of diamonds to a wall and expect it not to be seen by anyone?"

"That, Joyce," said Sammy, "is the million-dollar question."

CHAPTER ELEVEN

Root's Market looked strange, almost like a ghost town. The only thing missing was the lonesome wind blowing tumbling tumbleweeds between the buildings and around the empty outside stands. Four men could be seen rustling the litter from the day before. In the distance a vacuum machine howled, sucked up, and bagged yesterday's remnants. Wednesday was cleanup day at Root's.

The business office was inside building number one. It shared the same area as Bev's Snack Bar. Tom Longenecker, manager of the market, had his office in a partitioned-off area in a corner of the room.

Tom was thirty-eight, of medium height and weight, with well-trimmed dark blond hair and a mustache. On market days, Tuesdays, he displayed a tie and a businesslike attitude. On the other, less stressful days, he dressed casually. His moods were adjustable, depending on the situation. He had things well in hand.

When the three teenage detectives entered his office, Tom looked up and smiled. "I was just getting ready to call you. I have two pieces of information for you." He glanced down at a note on his desk. "Late yesterday afternoon after you left, a vender told me he was looking toward the parking lot earlier. He saw what he thought was a person, wearing a ski mask, grab a framed picture from a man with a white cane."

Brian's eyes opened wide. "Ha, serves them right," he said. "So our rip-off artists themselves were ripped off. Great!"

Ignoring Brian's emotional outburst, Sammy and Joyce looked at each other, exploring the possibilities of what the incident implied.

Finally, Sammy said, "We know Benny and the woman staged their little act for our benefit so Nick could steal the painting. A masked man shows up, so now we have a new player coming onto the scene."

"Just how many people are after the painting anyway?" asked Joyce.

"Evidently more than we realized," said Sammy. "Who else would know about the painting and its supposed link to the diamonds?" Then he remembered something he had heard yesterday at building nine when he had eavesdropped on Benny, Nick, and the woman. There was someone else in on the game. He was sure of it. But who?

"The second news I have for you," said Tom, "is we found the remains of your stolen painting."

"The remains?" said Sammy.

"Yeah, someone threw the painting into one of the trash cans and burned it. Do you want to see the ashes? We didn't empty the can yet."

"No," said Sammy, shaking his head, "we don't need to see it."

Brian saw the faint grin on Joyce's face. "Are you thinking what I'm thinking?" he asked.

"Probably," answered Joyce. "The masked man tore the painting apart, and when he didn't find anything, he got mad and threw it away."

"Why burn it?" asked Sammy, who was having trouble with Joyce's answer. "I can understand throwing the pieces away, but why take the trouble to burn them?"

"To destroy fingerprints," said Brian.

"No one's going to dust for prints on a worthless stolen painting," said Sammy.

"It's not worthless if it reveals the location of the diamonds," said Brian.

Sammy shook his head. "Even if he took the painting and figured out the coded message, I can't see him ending up burning it."

"Hey, if he figured out the dots on the dominoes, he went looking for the blockhouse," said Joyce.

"That's right," replied Brian. "Then Benny, Nick, and the woman went looking for him."

Sammy wanted to be sure he had all the bases covered. "Mr. Longenecker, has anyone approached you yesterday or today, asking about a house made of wooden blocks or logs?"

Tom shook his head. "No."

"Is there a house made of blocks here any-where?"

Tom didn't hesitate in answering. "Yes, we have one, only it's not made of wood."

All three teens stared in anticipation, their hearts racing.

"What's the house made of?" asked Joyce.

"Follow me. I'll show you."

The three excited amateur detectives hurried after Tom as he went outside. Ten feet from the front of the building, Tom suddenly stopped and pointed to his right. "There it is. We call it the 'blockhouse.'"

It was there all right, a real house, about twenty feet from where they stood. They were look-ing at it from the left side, near the back of the house. The house was made of blocks. Concrete blocks.

Sammy was thrilled. Was it going to be this easy? he wondered as he tried to take in all the details of the house.

The light gray, two-story building was large and had a wrap-around porch. Eight round concrete columns supported the porch roof. Two maple trees and six-foot evergreen shrubs grew in front. The rear of the house had an aluminum-siding addition. There were two back doors. One door was the rear entrance to the house; the other was a smaller door to the cellar. It was the smaller door that caught Sammy's attention.

Tom walked toward the back of the house. "Are you people still looking for the diamonds?" he asked.

Sammy, whose eyes were scanning the building for a quick and easy entry, said, "Yes, we are." He pointed and stepped toward the small door. "Is that door locked?"

"No, we don't lock it. It only goes to the cellar." Tom noticed the surprised look on their faces. "The police already searched it. You can't get up to the main house from there. It's just an underground cellar," he added. "Sometimes we store things there, but nothing of value."

"Are there any other easy accesses into the house?" asked Joyce.

"No, the doors are always locked as they were the day the cops chased the jewel thief through the market."

"May we have a look in the cellar?" asked Sammy.

"Sure, but as I said, the police have already searched down here," said Tom as he lifted the door latch and led the way down the old steps.

Brian was eager to enter the underground "tomb" and find the stolen jewels. His ever-perceptive senses were ready to hone in on the briefcase, no matter where it was hiding. Agent Helm, Brian Helm, otherwise known as double-oh-seven and a half, was ready to sniff it out. Hidden for over a year, surely the leather would give off a distinctive odor that Brian's super-sensitive sense of smell would spot and steer him to the spoils.

Brian positioned himself last in line—in case the others missed something on the way down. The darkness and dampness soon closed around them. Sparse light seeped in through casement windows. Brian wondered if it would have been better for him to wait outside—to be on the lookout for Benny, Nick, and the woman. He was going to suggest it to Sammy but changed his mind. His friend might get the wrong idea and think that he was scared. Imagine being scared of a little, old cellar. The worst that could happen would be spiders . . . mice . . . rats . . . a hand from a dead body ripping itself up through the dirt in the floor and grabbing . . . "Ahhhhh, no!" Brian screamed and fell into Joyce.

"What's wrong?" asked Joyce, trying to keep Brian from falling.

Brian looked down, expecting to see a hand. "I . . . I . . . tripped over something."

"Yeah, you're imagination," said Joyce.

"Here, let me turn on the light," said Tom.

A bare bulb supplied the needed light to navigate the isolated room.

As their eyes got accustomed to the light, the trio could make out pipes that ran across the ceiling and along two walls. The pipes were leading to and from water tanks, a water softener, and a furnace. A larger pipe carried sewage to the outside.

The detective team lost no time in searching the wall areas for any signs of a briefcase. They explored behind the pipes, the tanks, and the furnace. Sammy checked the wall behind the metal shelves which contained empty storage boxes. He inspected the pipes running across the ceiling. They could easily support a briefcase of diamonds should someone squeeze a leather case between the ceiling and the pipes.

Brian checked the floor for hidden trap doors and the walls for secret passages.

Nothing.

The high level of excitement, generated by the painting's secret message, evaporated into the damp, stale, underground air.

Then Sammy noticed that one of the four block walls was only six feet high, with pipes running over and beyond it. A two-foot opening existed from the top of the wall to the ceiling. Sammy stood on his toes and lifted his head, trying to glance over the top. Another small four feet by ten feet rectangular room existed beyond the wall.

Tom noticed the teen's interest. "That's the cistern, a room to catch and hold rainwater. Years ago the rain spouting outside gathered and channeled the rainwater into this storage area. At the time, the water was for household use. It's not used anymore."

"Hey," said Brian, "maybe the message meant 'over' the wall instead of 'on' the wall."

"May we look over?" asked Sammy.

Brian had already grabbed a three-foot stepladder from the corner.

"Ah, yeah. But as I said, the police were down here and looked in there," said Tom. "They even used that same stepladder."

Brian placed the stepladder against the wall, took three steps, and stood on the top platform. If he stood on his tiptoes, his head could lean over the top of the wall, and he could look down into the cistern. From that angle most of the cistern was visible.

"See anything on the walls?" asked Sammy, bracing Brian's legs to keep him from falling.

"No, just a foot or so of water at the bottom. No briefcase. No diamonds. Just plain block walls with clear water at the bottom." Brian pivoted around on top of the stepladder, looked down at the people below, and shrugged. "It's just a swimming pool that I wouldn't want to dive into."

Several things that were said bothered Sammy. He couldn't quite grasp the handle, but it was there. Something about the stepladder . . . the police . . . the walls . . . the briefcase on the wall. Then . . . "Brian, you said the walls were empty. Did you mean nothing was on any of the four walls?"

"Let me turn around and look again." He turned and stretched again so he could see over the wall and down to the water. "Yeah, there's nothing on the walls."

"Can you actually see the other side of the wall that you're looking over?" asked Sammy.

"Well, no," said Brian. "Hey, you're right. I can only see the other three walls, the two at the ends and the one opposite the wall I'm looking over. Wait till I hoist myself up." Brian lifted and stretched his left leg up to the top of the six-foot wall. He pulled himself up until his whole body was lying across the top. Now he could look over and see the other side of the wall that was under him. "It's here! It's here!" he yelled. He shimmied to position himself nearer the briefcase.

Everyone cheered. They had hit the jackpot. The diamonds were found.

"I can't believe this," said Tom. "Even the police looked and didn't see it."

"What's holding the briefcase to the wall?" asked Joyce.

Brian rested his right elbow on the concrete block and pointed ahead of him. "Do you see the wire running from that pipe, dropping down over the wall?"

"Yeah, I see it."

"The briefcase is dangling against the wall on the end of that wire," said Brian. "It's only about two feet down the wall." After slithering another several inches, Brian reached for the wire and pulled up. He flung the case over to the front side of the wall. Sammy reached up and grabbed it, being careful to hold it at the bottom. He untwisted the wire, trying not to disturb any fingerprints that might be on the handle.

Joyce guided Brian's feet back to the step-ladder as he lowered his body back down over the top edge of the wall.

"Well, open it. Open it," said Brian out of breath and brushing his hands down over his T-shirt and jeans.

Sammy, who was still gripping the briefcase by the bottom, nodded to Tom Longenecker. "Do you mind if we open it in your office? There's more light there."

"No, come on." Tom turned off the light and led the way up the steps.

The rest followed with Sammy bringing up the rear. He was holding the case in front with his arms extended straight out. Anyone observing the miniature parade marching from the "blockhouse" to the business office would think the teenager was carrying a bomb.

Once in the office, everyone positioned themselves around Tom's desk. Sammy gingerly lowered the hard-shell briefcase and laid it on its side. He took a tissue from his pocket and very carefully pressed each release button. Two chrome latches sprang up. He glanced at Brian and said, "Well, here goes." Using the tissue, he slowly raised the lid."

The others jockeyed for a better view of the diamonds. All eyes probed the opened case. Sammy lifted out the reinforced lining and searched for a false bottom. There was none.

Jubilation changed to sadness.

The case was indeed empty!

The diamonds were gone!

CHAPTER TWELVE

The first call went out to Detective Ben Phillips, who then called the Lancaster police. He reported that the briefcase connected to the Sidney Thomas case has been recovered but not the diamonds. The second call went to Fred Price, the retired salesman. Sammy had promised to call him if his briefcase was found.

As the police were interacting in Tom Longenecker's office, discussing the turn of events, the disappointed aspiring detectives sat outside the office at a table in Bev's deserted snack bar. They had given their statement to the police and were now conferring on who made off with the missing diamonds.

"I can't believe Benny, Nick, or the woman cracked the coded message," said Joyce.

"What if Benny knew beforehand that Sidney had used braille as the code, and all he needed was a close-up look at the painting?" asked Sammy.

"Couldn't he have seen it in jail or have taken a look at the painting on display before the auction started?" asked Joyce.

Brian swung his arm from left to right and then back again. "At the auction house they have a railing that keeps a distance between you and the items on the table. In jail, maybe Sidney kept Benny from seeing it, knowing that Benny knew braille."

"Remember, too," added Sammy, "that Benny is nearly blind. He needs to hold anything up close to see it. Even then it's probably a blur."

"So they steal the painting from us," said Brian, "break the code, find the briefcase, and take the diamonds."

"You're forgetting something," said Sammy. "Someone wearing a ski mask took the painting from them. So now we have another suspect thrown into the mix."

"Why leave the briefcase behind?" asked Joyce. "Here they are. They find the case full of diamonds. They spill the diamonds out into their pockets or into a box, reattach the wire to the case, and then, toss it back over the wall. Why take the time to do that?"

"Maybe they didn't want to be seen carrying the case," said Brian. "It was easier to carry the diamonds away in their pockets than in a bulky briefcase."

"But, what if they determined that the block-house was the house made of cinder block, and they discovered the unlocked back door," said Joyce. "They then decide that Sidney and the diamonds ended up in the cellar. Now, wouldn't they wait until dark last night to enter and to search the place? When they found the diamonds, they wouldn't need to ditch the case. They could walk away with it under the cover of darkness."

Fred Price entered the building, looked over at their table and then entered Tom's office. Sammy brushed his straight dark hair back from his eyes and watched through the glass windows as Fred introduced himself to the police.

"I think the masked man got the diamonds last night," said Brian.

Brian's remark brought Sammy's attention back to his friends. "Regardless of who, how, or why, with what we told the police, they'll keep an eye on Benny, Nick, and the woman and try to identify the masked man. You can be sure of that."

"What about Paul Brenner, who first got the painting at the auction? Any reason to suspect him?" asked Joyce.

"That's a good point, Joyce," said Sammy. "We can't be sure exactly when the diamonds were taken from the briefcase."

Before Sammy could continue, Brian said, "Right. What if Paul Brenner lied to us about his wife needing the vase. What if he was really after Sidney's painting all along. The vase was just a cover story."

"But you saw the two vases," said Sammy.

"Yeah, and how many more are there just like them?" asked Brian.

Joyce reached over and touched Sammy's arm. "I've never seen this Paul Brenner or the vases, but I like Brian's version."

Brian sat up tall in the chair, grinned, and added, "And as soon as Mr. Brenner got home that night, he and his wife figured out the braille message. He then threw the picture into his trash can, having no more need for it."

"I agree," said Sammy. "It is possible."

Fred Price left Tom's office and headed for the teenagers. He was not a happy man. He managed a smile as he extended his arm and shook hands with the young detectives. "I want to thank you for finding my briefcase. It was a present from my late wife. Did I tell you?"

They nodded.

Sadness returned to his eyes. "She was proud of me, you know. She . . ." He stopped and glanced back at the office. "I must wait until the police are done with my briefcase before it will be returned," he added.

Sammy had a sudden thought. "Mr. Price, as a traveling salesman, you probably contact a lot of local jewelry stores."

"Yes, more than I care to remember."

"There's a Dan Hall and his wife, Beth, who have a jewelry counter here at Roots. Were they one of your customers?" asked Sammy.

A small smile flashed on Fred's face. "Oh, yes, I've known Dan and his wife for years. Their D and D Jewelry Store is in the village of Fiddlers Green off the Lititz Pike. I wasn't aware they also had a stand here at the market on Tuesdays."

"I guess you get kind of friendly with some of your customers," suggested Sammy. "Go and eat lunch with them. That kind of thing."

"I usually don't have time for lunch, but I do joke around sometimes. I don't see what you're getting at."

"What I'm getting at is this. When chased by the police, Sidney Thomas headed here to Root's. Dan Hall and his D & D Jewelry stand is here. Maybe without knowing it, you gave information to Dan that helped pull off the robbery."

"Are you suggesting that Dan Hall was the mastermind behind the robbery?"

The young detective rubbed his hand down over his face. The frustration was getting to him. "No, I'm sorry. I'm just asking questions. That's all."

Brian was thinking about what Sammy had said. He looked his friend in the eye and asked, "You think Sidney Thomas gave the briefcase of diamonds to Dan Hall? Then do you think Mr. Hall's the one who slipped the diamond into my pocket?"

"Boys," said Joyce, "you're forgetting something. We found the briefcase hanging on the wall."

"Yeah, but it was empty," replied Brian. "Mr. Hall took the diamonds out of the case and then hid the case behind the wall."

"If that's true," said Joyce, "then his finger-prints will be of the latches." She moaned and added, "Unless he wiped them off."

"In which case we're right back to zero," said Brian.

"Well, not zero," said Joyce. "At least Mr. Price will get his briefcase back."

"That's a nice, heavy-duty case," said Sammy. "Did your wife buy it herself?"

Fred swallowed hard. "She did. The case was what she could afford at the time. I had it rein-forced to make it heavier," said Fred. "That's another reason I wanted it back. I'd really hate to lose it. Losing that case would be like losing part of my life. You teens are too young yet, but when you fall in love and get married, you'll understand about feelings, about caring, about sacrificing, about . . ." His voice faded away. He turn and waved good-bye before the teens could see the tears. He opened the door and left another building like he must have done thousands of times. Only now he wasn't carrying his briefcase.

The deep, sharp voice that interrupted the teens' picture of a departing, depressed man belonged to Detective Phillips. "Quite a letdown, finding the diamonds gone," he said. Then looking at Brian, he said, "I'm afraid your diamond is going to be one from the briefcase."

"How can they prove the diamond found in Brian's pocket is one of the stolen ones?" asked Joyce.

Phillips pulled a chair up to the table and sat. "The diamonds have no laser or other marking on them, so the only way to know is to find the rest of the diamonds. An inventory is always kept of the diamonds the salesmen carry. If the stolen diamonds are recovered, they'll check them against the inventory sheet. If a two-carat diamond is missing, then . . ." The detective raised his eyebrows and shrugged.

"Well, what do you think, Brian?" asked Sammy.

Brian wasn't so sure he wanted the diamonds found after hearing that. But then he had second thoughts. "Hey, I was supposed to be a big million-dollar sweepstakes winner. The letter said so. But I didn't wait at the door for the Brinks truck to show up. If I didn't do it for a million dollars, I'm certainly not going to be waiting for Detective Phillips to show up with a measly thirty-thousand-dollar diamond." Brian produced his widest artificial smile.

"Hey, I heard you almost found the diamonds," said Cheryl Zeiders as she approached the table.

"What are you doing here on a Wednesday? The market isn't open," said Sammy.

"After a hectic day like yesterday, I have to take a day to do some cleaning and straightening up." Cheryl glanced down and rubbed her hands over her dusty clothes.

Sammy recalled how Brian brushed himself after getting down from the wall. He also remembered that Cheryl was a nurse. "So you're not nursing today."

She looked at Sammy with that twinkle in her eye. "No, I don't have the 'patients.' That's a nurse joke," she added.

They all laughed.

Sammy decided to tell Cheryl about her stepbrother's painting so he could watch her reaction to the news. "Cheryl, the dominoes in Sidney's painting gave information on the location of the diamonds."

"I had no way of knowing," she said, looking surprised. "I can't believe I gave away a treasure map, showing where a million dollars in diamonds was hidden."

Sammy saw no signs of deceit in Cheryl's reaction. Of course, nurses were trained to nurture their patients. Was Cheryl masking her true feelings?

Ten minutes later, after the Lancaster detectives had gone and Sammy's father had arrived to take them home, Sammy made one more request of Detective Phillips. "Can you find out later from the Lancaster police if any fingerprints were found on the briefcase?"

"I will call them every hour on the hour," kidded Phillips, smoothing his mustache with several fingers. Then he turned serious, patted Sammy on the back, and said, "I'll call you as soon as I learn anything. I'm eager myself to know if any prints show up. If we're lucky, whoever took the diamonds from the case left his fingerprints behind."

"I'm not going to count on it," said Sammy. "I have a feeling there's more to this case than we know. Whoever it is, the 'mask' is out there laughing at us."

The "mask" wasn't laughing any more. Not now. Not since the bricfcase had been found. They weren't suppose to find it. Not before the "mask" found it. But now that the briefcase had been found, the "mask" would just have to sit and wait. He was hoping the meddling amateur detectives from Bird-in-Hand wouldn't figure it out.

CHAPTER THIRTEEN

The first thing they noticed was that the damaged back door and jamb had been replaced. No evidence remained of the break-in the week before. Sammy, Brian, and Joyce were hoping that Mary Brenner was home. They hadn't called first. Sammy got the idea for the visit as his father was driving them home from Root's. Sammy's father dropped them off, then went on to visit a business friend who lived nearby.

Sammy took a deep breath as he gently applied his knuckles to the door. He wanted to make one last visit before he eliminated the Brenners from his suspect list. And besides, Joyce said she wanted to see the two vases worth ten thousand dollars.

Mary Brenner answered on the first knock. This time she sported a wide smile as she opened the door and invited the teenage detectives inside.

Joyce took a liking to Mary right away. They had a lot in common, physically. They both were short, had the same wedge-type hair style, and dressed casually but neatly, everything in place. It was their areas of interest that differed. Joyce Myers loved photography, writing, and detective work; Mary Brenner was into antiques and history.

Sammy introduced Joyce then said, "Sorry we didn't call first, but we were on our way home and . . ."

"No problem," said Mary. "As you can see I have everything back in order. Come into the next room." She turned and soon they were faced with a room full of glass-door cabinets. "This is where I keep my vase collection," said Mary, stepping aside to provide a better view for her visitors.

Sammy counted eight cabinets, each numbered and each showing vases from a certain era in time. While the vases' shapes and designs were in full view, their history was not.

The display reminded Brian of his mother's doll collection. She, too, protected her collection behind glass doors. "Can you show Joyce the ten-thousand-dollar vases?" asked Brian.

"Sure, right here in cabinet number four," said Mary and pointed to the two centerpiece vases.

Brian nudged Sammy. "Number four. Another number," he said as a side remark.

"You'll have to excuse me for not taking them out of the cabinet," said Mary, "but I can't let anything happen to them."

Sammy thought that was odd. Mary had had the vases displayed on the kitchen table before.

"It's the history behind these two twin vases that makes them so valuable," explained Mary.

"They were made in England by Albert Spiegel for Lord Ashley of York. The twin vases were to be a birthday present for his wife, Lady Loran. His wife wanted two vases made, one to represent her husband, the other her. The two vases were to stand side by side forever."

"Collecting dust," said Brian.

"Oh, Brian, you're not romantic at all," said Joyce, punching him on his shoulder.

"In those days that was a romantic gesture," said Mary in a soft tone. In a harsher voice she added, "Today, the wife would want two cars sitting side by side in the garage, one for her and one for him."

They laughed.

Then Mary continued. "Anyway, Lord Ashley designed the two vases for his wife's birthday. Now in those days, one technique of applying a glaze to the pottery was to throw common table salt into the kiln. The soda from the salt created a glass coating to the vase's exterior."

"That's interesting," said Joyce. She glanced at Sammy. "We never did that when we made pottery at school. Did we?"

"No, it's news to me," answered Sammy.

"I think I knew it," said Brian. "That's why salt's bad for your heart. The glass builds up in your arteries and . . . well, you know the rest."

Mary cringed. She thought Brian was serious. Sammy and Joyce grinned. They knew it was Brian's way of getting attention.

"Now comes the mysterious part of the story," said Mary, returning her thoughts to the matching vases and their history. "When Lord Ashley had the vases made, he gave Albert Spiegel a handful of an unknown substance. Spiegel was to add the mysterious grains to the salt and the resulting mixture was to be put into the kiln along with the vases. The result was a pinkish glow that has never been duplicated to this day."

"You mean Lord Ashley wouldn't disclose the secret ingredient?" asked Brian.

"No," said Mary, "I mean, Lord Ashley died the next day. He took the secret with him to his grave."

The three young detectives moved closer to the cabinet. There was a unique pink brilliance to the vases. "I see what you mean," said Joyce as she squinted through the glass door of cabinet number four. "The vase's surface seems to pick up the light and intensifies it."

"Yep, and these are the only two," said Mary. "That's why they're worth ten thousand dollars."

"I'm curious," said Sammy. "How do you know that story is true?"

"I stumbled across it accidentally one time, doing research in a library in England. It was mentioned in an old book titled, *Romantic Overtures*. It had a drawing of the two vases. I didn't think much of it until later when Paul and I were vacationing in Canada."

"Is that where you got the first vase?" asked Joyce.

"Yeah, an antique dealer had it, along with a copy of the story about the vases. He said he'd been trying to get its mate but was unsuccessful. So he sold the vase to me."

Mary was bombarded with three sets of inquiring eyes that wanted to know.

"Three hundred dollars," she replied, answering their nonverbal question.

"That makes for a hefty profit. Don't you think?" asked Paul Brenner, who had been listening at the doorway.

Sammy ignored Mr. Brenner's question. Instead he asked one himself. "I heard you were at Root's Country Market yesterday. Do you have a stand there?"

Paul glanced at Joyce. "I haven't met you yet." He extended his hand.

Joyce introduced herself as she shook his hand. She added, "I go to school with Sammy and Brian."

"I'll tell you this," said Paul. "You're traveling in good company. By the way, I've heard you're quite a detective yourself."

Joyce blushed from the compliment.

Paul peered at Sammy. "Who told you I was at Root's on Tuesday?"

"I was talking to Cheryl Zeiders. She mentioned it," said Sammy.

"Good old Cheryl. If you're ever sick, she's the nurse you want. She has that something special. You know what I mean?"

Sammy smiled. "Yeah, that twinkle in her eye."

Brian ignored the "small talk" going on. He had his nose pressed against the glass door, looking for the cosmic glow radiating from the vases. He couldn't see it.

"No, I don't have a stand at Root's," said Paul finally. "I go looking for antiques. I spend most of my time at the Conestoga Auction across the road. How did your plans with the painting work out? Did the woman and the others show up?"

The three amateur detectives watched Paul and Mary as Sammy unfolded the events of Tuesday and that morning. He ended with, "The police are checking the empty briefcase for fingerprints."

Paul Brenner and his wife looked at each other, seemingly surprised. "The painting was responsible for someone finding the diamonds," said Mary. "A masked man got the painting and burned it." She glanced at Brian. "One of the stolen diamonds turned up in your pocket. That's fantastic. I can't believe it. I thought stuff like that only happens in mystery novels."

Before anyone could respond to Mary's comment, a loud knock came from the back door. It was Sammy's father, wanting to know if the teens were ready to go home. He was invited inside, shown the two vases, and then after ten minutes of social talk, they were in the car driving back to Bird-in-Hand.

Since it was early afternoon, Sammy's father treated them each to a sandwich at the Bird-in-Hand Family Restaurant. After they ate, the trio agreed to meet in Sammy's room at seven o'clock for a much-needed brainstorming session.

🔻 🔻 🔻 🔻

The black spot moving erratically across the ceiling caught Joyce's eye. She continued to rock at a steady pace while waiting for Brian to settle back on the bed. Finally, without waiting any longer, she kicked her right foot against the bed and pointed. "Hey, isn't that Larry up there?"

Any spider on the ceiling or wall was Brian's make-believe spider friend, Larry. Brian really hated spiders, but he didn't want his human friends to know. Anytime a spider came into view, he always had something to say about "Larry."

Brian flinched at first, but when he saw the spider at a safe distance from him on the ceiling, he smiled. "Yep, that's my friend, Larry."

Sammy was always trying to stump his best friend, or to see what story Brian could come up with. "You amaze me, Brian. How do you know that's Larry?" he asked.

"Oh, I can tell by . . . by . . . by the way he walks."

"Oh?" said Sammy. "You can tell by his walk."

"How can you do that?" asked Joyce, joining Sammy in trying to pin Brian to the wall.

"Yeah," added Sammy as he winked at Joyce, "All spiders have eight legs. I thought all spiders walked pretty much the same way."

The grin on Brian's face showed he was not about to let his friends trap him. "Larry's left front leg is shorter than the rest," he answered.

"And?" said Sammy.

"Well, the short leg adds a dip to his walk. When you see a spider that dips, you know it's Larry."

"Are you saying Larry's kind of dippy," said Joyce, giggling.

"Yeah, that short leg throws the other seven legs out of sync. You know, it just throws off their timing. It creates a mess. Sometimes he ties up traffic for hours. Nobody wants to walk behind him."

"But every time I see Larry, he's always alone," said Sammy.

"See? Now you know why." Brian was smiling at the ceiling.

"Brian, explain this," said Sammy, pulling his chair from behind his desk to get a better view of his friend. "Larry lived on my bedroom ceiling across the street before we moved over here. How did he get across the street, one block down? And don't tell me he walked over," added Sammy to shorten the options for Brian.

The rocking chair came to a halt. Joyce leaned forward. She wanted to hear this.

Silence.

"Well?" asked Sammy.

Brian's eyes were still on the spider creeping across the ceiling. He sighed. "It's a sad story," he said. "You probably don't want to hear it."

"Oh, no, we definitely want to hear it," said Joyce, making a face at Sammy.

Brian's voice quivered as he said, "It was a very traumatic experience for Larry. I don't think I should repeat it in front of him. It's, it's, it's a very sad, emotional story. I cry every time I think about it."

"Spiders must confront their fears," said Sammy. "It's beneficial therapy for them. It says so in my psychology books."

"Tell us about it," said Joyce, "so Larry can relive the experience and become free of all anxiety and fear."

"Oh, sure, it'll do Larry a lot of good, but how about me?" asked Brian. He paused and saw that Sammy and Joyce were not going to let up. He had to continue. His pride said so. "Okay, you asked for it. Once upon a time . . ." Brian started.

"Forget the frills, Brian. Get to the story," said Sammy.

"Okay, okay. It was fourteen days after your family moved their business over to this side of the street that—"

"Two weeks," said Joyce.

"What?" asked Brian.

"Fourteen days is two weeks. You should say two weeks not—"

"Spiders don't reckon time in weeks. They only consider days."

"Okay, it was fourteen days after we moved," said Sammy. "Continue."

"Larry cried every day I was gone. I get a knot in my throat just thinking about it," said Brian. "He cried and cried and cried and cried—"

"Brian," said Sammy.

"But it was fourteen days," explained Brian.

"What did Larry do on the fourteenth day?" asked Sammy. By this time both he and Joyce wanted to hear how Brian was going to get out of this.

"In the meantime, a new business and a new family had moved in. There was no one to replace me. Poor Larry sobbed his way from your old bedroom ceiling to the ceiling downstairs in the store. He waited until a woman asked directions to the Bird-in-Hand Country Store. He dropped down onto her head, thinking she would carry him over to your parents' new shop. Then it's a hop, skip, and a jump to come up here."

"That was smart of Larry," said Joyce.

"Well, as it turned out, it wasn't," replied Brian, sliding his hands behind his head. "When the woman got to the car, her husband said they had to leave Bird-in-Hand and go home."

"Boy, Larry's in trouble now," said Joyce, shaking her head and grinning at Sammy.

"You can't imagine how much," said Brian, his hands lifting his head from the bed. "The people were from Canada."

Joyce raised her hand to her mouth. "Oh, my. How is poor Larry going to get out of this?" she said melodramatically.

"Yeah, I wonder," said Brian, having no idea where he was going with his little tale of woe.

"I can see how this would be a difficult moment for Larry," said Sammy.

"It wasn't as bad as you might think," said Brian, thinking fast. "The people from Canada stopped for lunch at Alex Austin's Steakhouse in Smoketown."

"That was a bit of luck," said Sammy, scratching his cheek.

"As it turned out, it wasn't," said Brian. "They parked their car in the parking lot. As the woman got out of the car, her head brushed against the door frame, flipping Larry down to the car seat."

"So Larry's trapped in the car," said Sammy. "Too bad."

"No, it wasn't bad at all," said Brian. "The door window was open, so Larry crawled out and jumped down to the ground."

"I hate to ask this, but is that good?" asked Joyce.

Brian's neck was hurting so he sat up. "No, not good at all because a boy on a bicycle came riding by."

"Oh, oh," said Joyce, overacting. "Now Larry's in real trouble."

"No, not really." Brian puffed out his chest and grinned. "For you see, that boy was me."

"That's rather poetic, Brian," said Sammy, "and such a happy ending."

"That's not exactly the end," said Brian sadly, drawing his moment of glory out as long as possible. "Larry was in the path of my bike, and, sad to say, I didn't see him."

"Oh, my, Larry's in for it now," said Joyce, spreading her arms wide.

"No, as luck had it, Larry saw the danger he was in and started to run."

"You recognized Larry's running dip and applied your brakes just in time to rescue poor, old Larry," said Sammy, standing and applauding with Joyce joining in.

"Yep, I saved my friend, Larry, from certain doom and brought him up here to be with me, forever."

After the cheering and the clapping subsided, Sammy glanced up and saw that that the spider had disappeared from the ceiling. "Larry's not up on the ceiling any more, Brian. I think he dropped down on your head."

"What?" Brian's head snapped up, his eyes scanned the ceiling. "Oh, no!" His head tipped forward, his hands whipped at his hair to remove anything that might be crawling there.

Sammy and Joyce grinned as they watched Brian doing the spider dance.

While Brian was regaining his composure, Sammy glanced at his watch. "Enough time for fun. Let's get back to serious business," he said as he returned to his chair and snapped up the 8x10 photos that still remained on his desk. "We have to pick up the bits and pieces. Now that the diamonds have been stolen twice, I'm afraid the trail is getting thinner and thinner."

The rocking chair creaked back and forth, reflecting Joyce's irritation at the hopelessness of the case. "The easiest way for this case to end," said Joyce, "would be for the culprit's fingerprints to show up on the briefcase."

Sammy reflected on that thought. "Except for Sidney Thomas and Fred Price. Their prints are expected to be there. The police took Brian's and my prints this morning to eliminate them if they turned up on the briefcase."

Brian had inspected the bed before he repositioned himself comfortably and was now staring at the ceiling, wondering where the spider had gone. "Right," he said. "It's a good thing I didn't touch the case when I pulled it up over the wall."

Both Sammy and Joyce didn't say it, but they were thinking the same thing. If Brian's fingerprints were found on the briefcase, the evidence would point to him as the thief because of the diamond found in his pocket.

Sammy shuffled through the rest of the photos that Joyce had taken while standing on the table at Root's Country Market. He stopped at one picture. He recognized someone. A lone figure was standing in a recessed corner between two stands. The eyes appeared to be riveted on something. Sammy followed the line of sight and stopped at three familiar folks, Benny, Nick and the woman. The figure was apparently watching Nick doing something to the white cane. If a puzzle had a keystone piece, this would be it. This was the puzzle piece that held the others together. "Come look at what we have here!" he cried out.

Those words were words of hope to Brian and Joyce. They both jumped up and hurried behind the desk.

"We're not done with this case yet. Right, Sammy?" said Brian as his eyes scooted over the photo. "Hey, there are our friends, the Three Stooges."

"Yeah, but look over here," said Sammy, pointing at the edge and smiling. He was beginning to see the light at the end of the tunnel.

"I recognize the person," said Joyce, "but I don't see—"

Sammy interrupted. "What had me puzzled was, a person shows up in a ski mask to steal the painting. It's July. Where did the ski cap come from?"

"The guy's a thief," said Brian. "Why wouldn't he have a mask?"

Sammy pondered Brian's statement. "I don't think the thief came to Root's with the ski mask to get Sid's painting. After all, the painting was there to be sold—until I had told Nick that it was already sold. It was after that moment that the painting was up for grabs." Sammy pointed to the photo. "Here's Nick preparing the cane so he can snatch the painting from the pole."

"So the big question is," said Joyce, "who, after seeing what Nick was planning with the white cane, was able to come up with a ski mask that fast? But I still don't see how—"

"Sammy! Phone!" came the voice from down-stairs.

"That should be Detective Phillips with the fingerprint report," said Sammy. He handed the photo to Brian and then vanished down the stairs.

Brian studied the picture again and frowned. He picked up the other photos. Each 8x10 showed people eating, shopping, and traveling from one stand to another. Sure, he saw some people he knew, but he didn't get it. What's the big deal about the ski mask? He looked at Joyce who just shrugged and shook her head.

Sammy came barreling up the steps. "Okay, we're ready to go."

"Where are we going?" asked Brian.

"We're going to unmask a jewel thief," replied Sammy.

CHAPTER FOURTEEN

Twilight painted a soft shadowy, suburban countryside, complete with ranch houses, flowers, trees, and space. Two unmarked police cars quietly entered the serene picture. They pulled up and parked across the road a hundred feet from one of the houses. From there, the front and the back of the property could be observed. In the lead car was Detective Dan Withers, Lancaster City police. The second car held Detective Ben Phillips, Bird-in-Hand police, and three teenage, novice detectives. One of the amateur detectives had a cellular phone in his hand.

Earlier, when Detective Phillips reported the fingerprint results, Sammy figured he was right. While still on the phone with Phillips, he laid out his theory as to who committed the robbery and detailed a plan for proving it. Phillips was so impressed with Sammy's logic, he contacted his friend, Detective Withers, who arranged a stake-out. Since the diamond robbery occurred in

Lancaster, it was in the hands of the Lancaster police. Phillips was dressed leisurely and tagged along as an off-duty policeman. Sammy, Brian, and Joyce were there as concerned citizens—with a plan.

Detective Withers was in his thirties, a tall man with sandy hair. Under the business suit he wore was a gun. That's the part that meant business. He spotted a car in the driveway and a light coming from the front window. "Someone's home," he said into the mike he was holding. He added, "Go ahead. Let's start the ball rolling."

Phillips received the message. He glanced back at the three young detectives in the back seat. "Okay, Sammy, it's up to you now."

As Sammy started to push buttons, a car pulled into the driveway. A man dashed out of the car, stormed toward the house, and pounded at the door.

"Hold it," said Phillips as he grabbed for the mike. "Do you see that, Dan?"

"Yeah, we have a late arrival," said Withers.

Everything happened so fast, but Joyce was ready with her camera. She zoomed in and focused just as the front door opened. The light from inside reached the man. It was enough for Joyce to snap a shot and to identify the visitor.

"It's Nick Palmer," she said.

Before anyone could comment, a heated argument, originating in the house, was loud enough to be heard on the outside.

"It sounds like Nick Palmer figured it out," said Sammy.

"The sparks are flying in there," said Detective Withers into his mike. "Let's still go with the plan. This sounds like a good time."

"I agree," said Phillips. "Okay, Sammy, make your call."

The shouting continued in the house. The pot was boiling. That pleased Sammy. He hoped his plan would cause the pot to boil over and run. He had no strong evidence, but there were many small truths that pointed to only one person. He dialed the memorized number and waited.

The phone rang.

The shouting stopped.

The phone rang again.

"Hello," said a suspicious voice.

"Hello, this is Sammy Wilson. I want you to know that we figured it out. We know who stole the diamonds. In exactly one hour from now, I am going to call the police and tell them what I know. I just thought I'd tell you first." Sammy pushed the END button and handed the phone back to Phillips.

Phillips nodded. "Now we wait."

The somber colors left by the fading twilight only enhanced the uncertainty of the moment. It was like sky diving—you counted on the parachute to open. Sammy was counting on the action to start. He had pulled the rip cord; now he wanted to see what unfurled.

Sammy's plan was based on the theory that when exposed, the guilty person would make a run for it—with the stolen diamonds. The only way for Sammy's plan to be successful was to catch the guilty party with the diamonds. There was no other tangible evidence.

A nearby street light came on and challenged the oncoming darkness, spoiling the mystique. And then, as though the artificial illumination announced, "lights, camera, action," it happened.

Two figures emerged from the back of the house. One carried a shovel.

Joyce pointed her camera. The zoom lens captured close-ups as the figures roamed across the yard and selected a spot.

The shovel dug deep, judging from the number of times it assaulted the hole. Finally, the shovel was flung aside. One figure knelt at the hole, reached, and lifted what appeared to be a coffee can.

"This is it. Let's do it," announced Withers' voice from the speaker.

Detective Withers took the lead, crossing the road and hurrying over the lawn. Phillips and the young detectives tagged behind.

The two figures were so engrossed in the coffee can that they were surprised to find themselves suddenly surrounded by an audience.

Detective Withers dangled his ID in front of two very shocked faces. "I'm the police, Detective Dan Withers. I'm sorry, but I must detain you two for a while."

"Hey, I have nothing to do with this," said Nick Palmer. "I'm just visiting."

Their eyes centered on the other person.

"What's this all about?" asked Fred Price as he lowered the coffee can and tried to hide it behind him.

"Both of you, down on the ground on your stomach," demanded Withers. "Spread your hands and feet."

Price was still holding the can as he flopped on the ground. "Why are you doing this?" he asked, releasing the can and causing it to roll away. The can clinked and clanged and rattled and rolled.

"Does that sound like reason enough?" asked Sammy.

"By any chance, could that mysterious sound we hear be the stolen diamonds?" asked Detective Withers. He patted Fred Price down for weapons while Phillips searched Nick Palmer.

Whatever hope Fred Price had for his future was now gone. He knew the grand plan for a brighter tomorrow was over. He proved to himself once again that he was a failure. He had made the wrong choices.

"It's over," said Phillips as he picked up the can and opened it. He smiled. "These look like diamonds to me," he said, tilting the can for Withers to see.

The super sleuths watched as Detective Withers snapped the handcuffs on Fred Price and Nick Palmer, stood them up, and read them their rights.

With his hands shackled behind him, Price stared at Sammy. "How did you know?"

"When I overheard Nick here talking to Benny Hayes and the woman outside building nine at Root's, I knew a third person was involved in the robbery."

"You were there? Why? What did I say?" asked Nick.

"You said that you were all to get an even share of the diamonds. Your share was to be one-third. One-third. That meant three people were involved in the original robbery."

"But how did you know I was the third person?" asked Price.

"It was a series of things," answered Sammy. "The photo taken by Joyce showed you watching Benny, Nick, and the woman, with Nick working on the cane. You knew they were up to something. When you came and talked to us at the stand, you saw the painting on the pole. It didn't take you long to figure out what Nick was going to do with the cane."

"But that doesn't mean anything," said Price.

"You told us at Root's that you carry things in your car to disguise yourself so would-be jewel thieves wouldn't recognize you. In the wintertime when it's freezing cold, I bet a ski cap comes in handy." Sammy pointed to a car in the driveway. "When the police search your car, what are the chances they'll find a ski cap there among your fake beard, wigs, and clothing?"

Fred said nothing. He just shook his head.

"You went to your car and got the ski cap. You watched and when Nick hooked the painting with the cane, you followed him. You slipped the ski mask over your face so Nick wouldn't recognize you. Then you burned the painting to destroy it."

"Why would I want to destroy the painting?"

"That had me stumped for a while," said Sammy. "Yes, why was the painting destroyed? My guess is, you probably took the painting apart and found no directions to the diamonds. In case you had missed something, you burned the pieces so no one else could examine it. Under no circumstances did you want the briefcase found."

"He wanted to be the first one to find it. Right, Sammy?" said Brian.

"It was very important that he be the first person to find it," said Sammy.

Brian looked puzzled. "Why?"

"Because if the police got to the briefcase first, both the police and Nick would come looking for Mr. Price."

Brian was confused. "Why would they do that?"

Sammy nodded toward Fred Price. "It was because of the secret—the big secret that only Fred Price knew. Even your two partners didn't know. Did they Mr. Price?"

With his hands handcuffed behind him, Nick lunged at Fred Price, knocking him off balance.

Withers's grasp kept him from falling. "You scum," said Nick. He spit on Fred and yelled, "We trusted you, and you tricked us! Sid died for nothing!" Nick looked toward Sammy. "I figured out the secret today. That's why I'm here."

"What was the big secret?" asked Brian.

"The briefcase that Sidney Thomas grabbed in the staged robbery was empty. There never were any diamonds in the briefcase."

It took awhile for that idea to sink in.

"You see," said Sammy, "the diamonds were supposed to be in the briefcase, but Mr. Price kept them for himself. Sidney had grabbed an empty briefcase."

"But couldn't Sidney tell by the weight that the case was empty?" asked Brian.

"The answer to that gave me another reason to suspect Mr. Price. Remember when I commented on the briefcase being heavy-duty? Mr. Price said he had had the case reinforced and made heavier. But why? Earlier he told us, if a thief really wanted to get at the diamonds, he could find a way to get them. So why add extra weight to a case he would have to lug around day after day? No, the extra thickness was added to make up for the weight of the missing diamonds."

"How did you know that someone didn't find the case hanging on the wall and take the diamonds?" asked Brian.

"Because Fred Price's fingerprints were found on the chrome latches."

"But even you opened the case, using a tissue so as not to disturb any prints that might be on it. Someone else could have done the same thing."

"Yes, but I didn't use the tissue on the chrome latches to close the case. If I had, Fred Price's fingerprints would have been smeared or at least slightly blurred. When Detective Phillips told me the prints found on the latches belonged to Mr. Price and were crisp and clear, it meant Mr. Price was the last person to close the briefcase. The absence of diamonds in the case meant that Fred Price had closed an empty briefcase. He had pocketed the diamonds for himself."

Nick sneered. "The diamonds were supposed to be in the case the day Sid and I took it from him. You double-crossing . . ." Nick stopped his verbal assault on Fred and gritted his teeth.

"That's why he was anxious to get his case back," said Joyce. "It wasn't because of his wife. It was because he knew his fingerprints would still be on the latches."

"But the case wasn't locked," said Brian. "Wouldn't Sidney Thomas discover the case was empty when he opened it later?"

"Maybe we better look to Mr. Price for the answer to that one," said Sammy.

All eyes riveted on Fred.

He spoke softly. "When you're traveling day after day, you have time to think. I took my time and I planned what I thought was a perfect jewel heist. I arranged for Sid and Nick to help with the plan. They thought they would get one third of the diamonds. Sidney was to take the briefcase of diamonds to his parents' cabin and hide them. After two years when the heat was off, we would all take our share and go our own way."

"Your plan, however, called for you to disappear with all the diamonds before the two years were up," said Phillips.

Fred Price nodded. "Now, how did I know Sidney wouldn't open the briefcase and find it empty? We didn't trust each other, so to make sure nobody opened the case before we all got together in two years, I told them I would place a red-stain bomb inside with the diamonds. That meant if anyone opened the case before I was there to disarm it, the bomb would explode, covering anybody and everything with a red dye."

"Even that was a lie," said Nick. "There was nothing in the case."

"Your plan fell apart," said Joyce, "when someone reported the robbery and the police caught up with Sidney at Root's."

"With the police after him, Sidney headed for Root's because his stepsister, Cheryl, was there," suggested Sammy. "Sidney thought he'd get her to hide the diamonds for him. Instead, she turned him down, and so Sidney was forced to find another hiding place. He stumbled across the unlocked 'blockhouse' cellar door, hooked a wire to the handle, and threw the case over the cistern wall."

Brian pointed a finger at Price. "You put the diamond in my pocket. Right?"

Fred Price nodded. "I wanted you to think the diamonds were found so you'd stop looking for the case."

Joyce was confused. "You had the diamonds all the time. Why didn't you just walk away with them after the robbery when the briefcase got lost at Root's Country Market?"

"My retirement," replied Fred.

"Your retirement?" asked Joyce. "I don't understand."

"In a jewel heist like mine, the first person the insurance investigators suspect is the salesman. I knew they would check me out. My record is clean and they had no evidence to point to me as being involved in the robbery. As long as I led a normal life, I was in the clear. But if I was to vanish right after the robbery, the police would come after me. I'm too old. I didn't want to live out my remaining days always looking over my shoulder."

"What does your retirement have to do with it?" asked Brian.

"I retire next month. By waiting until I retire, I could just walk away from my job, collect social security, and go on a vacation with no questions asked. I had intended to resettle in another state where Sid and Nick couldn't find me. I figured they would be mad when they finally opened the case and found it empty."

Joyce shook her head. "Why did you steal the diamonds in the first place? Did you really need the money that badly?"

Joyce's words ignited an emotional outburst from Fred Price. "I gave my whole life to the jewelry business. I made millions for them. What do I get in return? Headaches, a bad back, flat feet, and social security. My wife died. I have no children. I have nothing. I deserved more."

"The judge will see that you get it—room and board paid by the taxpayers," said Phillips. He had no sympathy for these whiners. Millions of people are in the same boat, but they don't conspire to steal from others. He grabbed Nick Palmer and nodded to Withers. "Come on. I'll help you load these two into your car. I have to get my three friends home, or I'll have to arrest myself for having them out past curfew."

Detective Withers thanked Ben Phillips for his help and congratulated Sammy, Brian, and Joyce on the clever detective work they had performed to solve the case.

♦ ♦ ♦

Fifteen minutes later, driving toward Bird-in-Hand on the Old Philadelphia Pike, Joyce unexpectedly said, "Pull in here, please. If you don't mind."

Phillips didn't know what to expect, but he managed to pull into the parking lot of an antique shop.

"What's up?" asked Sammy.

"I'll be right back," said Joyce. "Oh, and while I'm gone, take a look." She pointed to the antique shop window.

After the shock wore off, the boys started to laugh. In the window was a vase exactly like Mary Brenner's two vases. Detective Phillips didn't get the joke until Sammy explained the story of the twin vases which now somehow became triplets.

When Joyce returned to the car, she asked with a smile, "Guess who just got back from Canada and has a vase and a story to sell?"

"Could it possibly be that antique dealer?" asked Brian jokingly, pointing to the shop.

"He's willing to sell the vase for five hundred dollars along with the certified story that goes with it," said Joyce.

"Did you tell him the truth?" asked Brian. "That the dealer in Canada is running a scam."

"No, I didn't have the heart."

Phillips backed out of the driveway and headed east again.

"So the vases are worthless," said Brian. "Wait until Mary Brenner hears this."

"I don't think Mary wants to hear it," said Sammy. "She's content to believe."

"Yeah, and she wasn't the only one who saw the extra glow from the glaze," said Brian, pointing to Joyce.

"But I did see light coming from the vases," admitted Joyce.

"I noticed that the cabinet had lights that spotlighted the vases," said Sammy. "Maybe that explains it."

"You see, that's it right there," said Brian. "It's what I always say, 'The brighter the light, the less you can see.'"

Sammy and Joyce stared at each other. "But if there's no light, you can't see either," said Joyce, trying to confuse Brian.

"You definitely need light to see, Brian," said Sammy, adding to the confusion.

Brian pleaded, "But too much of a good thing can . . ."

"Can what?" asked Sammy.

"Like if you eat too much food, you can get sick."

"Not if you eat slowly," added Joyce.

"It doesn't matter at what speed you eat. You can get sick if you eat too much," said Brian, raising his voice.

"Then why do you want to eat too much?" asked Sammy.

"I don't want to eat too much. I . . . Ah, forget it," said Brian. He tapped Phillips on the shoulder. "You can let me off here. I'll walk the extra block. I need time away from these two."

Phillips grinned. Ah, to be young again, he thought to himself as he pulled over and stopped.

Brian got out of the car, said good-bye, and watched his friends drive away. He saw the car getting smaller and smaller. He tugged at his pants, and headed for home. The darkness closed in around him. He was alone.

He sighed.

He missed his friends already. He didn't need light to see that.

Sammy was wrong.

SAMMY AND BRIAN MYSTERY SERIES

#1 **The Quilted Message** by Ken Munro

The whole village was talking about it. Did the Amish quilt contain more than just twenty mysterious cloth pictures? The pressure was on for Bird-in-Hand's two teen-age detectives, Sammy and Brian, to solve the mystery. Was Amos King murdered because of the quilt? Who broke into the country store? It was time for Sammy and Brian to unmask the intruder. $4.95

#2 **Bird in the Hand** by Ken Munro

When arson is suspected on an Amish farm, the village of Bird-in-Hand responds with a fund-raiser. The appearance of a mysterious tattooed man starts a series of events that ends in murder. And who is The Bird? Sammy and Brian are bound hand and foot by the feathered creature. Bird-in-Hand's own teenage sleuths break free and unravel the mystery. $5.95

#3 **Amish Justice** by Ken Munro

The duo turns into a trio when Joyce Myers becomes the newest member of the Sammy and Brian detective team. Is farmland in Lancaster County worth killing for? Frank Crawford thinks so. And when the police call the attempts on his life accidents, the old farmer sends for the teenage detectives. The three sleuths soon discover one of five suspects knows about the "IT" under the house. $5.95

#4 **Jonathan's Journal** by Ken Munro

After Scott Boyer comes to town, a young girl disappears. He then makes an offer Sammy and Brian can't refuse. A 200-year-old journal holds a challenge of a life-time. It holds two secrets: a mysterious puzzle and murder. Bird-in-Hand's super detectives investigate the meaning behind its cryptic message. $5.95

#5 **Doom Buggy** by Ken Munro

An Amish buggy disappears. Twenty cut-out letters appear in its place. Then some-one wants George Brock dead—in his welding shop. Sammy, Brian, and Joyce, fifteen-year-old sleuths from Bird-in-Hand, try to find the connection between these three mysterious happenings. $5.95

#6 **Fright Train** by Ken Munro

The actor, John Davenport, retires in Strasburg. He brings with him Manaus, the monster from his cult movie, *Fright Train*. While riding the Strasburg Railroad, Sammy and Brian learn that someone wants to steal something from the actor. But what? Is it his autobiography manuscript? Or is it the "Fright Train"? $5.95

#7 **Creep Frog** by Ken Munro

Where in Kitchen Kettle Village is Charles Parker? The frog isn't talking, but Zulu, the African parrot, has plenty to say. Charles Parker is masquerading under a new identity in Kitchen Kettle Village. U.S. Marshals want Sammy and Brian to find their hidden witness before Mack Roni, a thug, finds him. The frog is kidnapped, but why? And—will someone kiss the frog and turn him into Charles Parker? $5.95

— —

These books may be purchased at your local bookstore or ordered from Gaslight Publishers, P. O. Box 258, Bird-in-Hand, PA 17505.

Enclosed is $_____(please add $2.00 for shipping and handling). Send check or money order only.

Name_____

Address_____

City————————————————— State ————— Zip Code——————————